the
yadayada
Prayer Group®
GETS DECKED OUT

Other novels in the Yada Yada series:

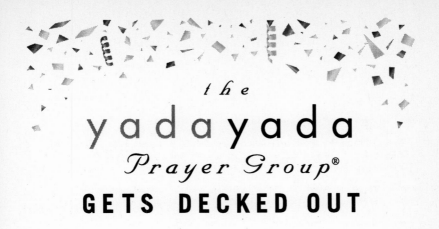

the

yadayada

Prayer Group®

GETS DECKED OUT

a Novel

neta jackson

THOMAS NELSON
Since 1798

NASHVILLE   DALLAS   MEXICO CITY   RIO DE JANEIRO

Published in Nashville, Tennessee by Thomas Nelson. Thomas Nelson is a registered trademark of Thomas Nelson, Inc.

Published in association with the literary agency of Alive Communications, Inc., 7680 Goddard Street, Suite 200, Colorado Springs, CO 80920.

Thomas Nelson, Inc. titles may be purchased in bulk for educational, business, fund-raising, or sales promotional use. For information, please e-mail SpecialMarkets@ThomasNelson.com.

Scripture quotations are taken from the following: THE HOLY BIBLE, NEW INTERNATIONAL VERSION® (NIV). Copyright © 1973, 1978, 1984 by International Bible Society. Used by permission of Zondervan. All rights reserved.

The Holy Bible, New Living Translation, copyright © 1996, 2004. Used by permission of Tyndale House Publishers, Inc., Wheaton, Illinois 60189. All rights reserved.

The New King James Version®. Copyright © 1982 by Thomas Nelson, Inc. Used by permission. All rights reserved.

This novel is a work of fiction. Any references to real events, businesses, organizations, and locales are intended only to give the fiction a sense of reality and authenticity. Any resemblance to actual persons, living or dead, is entirely coincidental.

Library of Congress Cataloging-in-Publication Data

Jackson, Neta.
   The yada yada prayer group gets decked out / Neta Jackson.
      p. cm.
     ISBN-13: 978-1-59554-361-5 (pbk.)
     ISBN-10: 1-59554-361-9 (pbk.)
     1. Women—Illinois—Fiction. 2. Prayer groups—Fiction. 3. Female friendship—Fiction. 4. Christian women—Fiction. 5. Chicago (Ill.)—Fiction. I. Title.
    PS3560.A2415Y3335 2007
    813'.54—dc22

                          2007045990

Printed in the United States of America

10 11 12 13 EPAC 12 11 10 9 8

For Dave

without whose love, patience, encouragement,
and takeover of the Jackson kitchen
this novella would never be

Prologue

*T*he steady *ding-a-ling* of the Salvation Army bell down the street punctuated the Christmas lust of the three boys gawking into the window of the game store. "Look, they got PlayStation Portable! That's what I want, man. 'Member those ads we saw on TV, JJ? *Awesome* graphics."

"Ha! Look how much it cost. That PSP is over two hundred bucks! How you gonna get that, Boomer?"

Boomer, almost as tall as his thirteen-year-old cousin even though he was two grades younger, shrugged inside his bulky jacket. "I dunno. Ask for it for Christmas. Why not?"

The older boy snorted. "Yeah, right. Yo' mama ain't gonna spring for no two hundred bucks. 'Specially when she finds out you ain't home, *grounded* like she said when you cut class yesterday."

"She ain't gonna find out 'less *you* tell her, JJ. She at work."

The third boy snickered.

Boomer glared at his cousin's friend. "Don't you start, Mitch. C'mon, let's go in. I wanna check out the new games."

The three middle school boys pushed their way into the crowded store, jackets unzipped, knit caps pulled over their ears, wet gym shoelaces dragging. The week after Thanksgiving had followed early winter's treacherous trend: first a drizzling rain, then freezing temperatures, then a light snow to dust the icy sidewalks and streets. Shoppers filled the aisles of the game store, even though it was a weeknight. With only "24 Shopping Days till Christmas," stores were open all over Chicago until ten at night, every night.

Boomer pulled back the hood of his sweatshirt layered under his sport jacket as he paused in front of the big display featuring the new game console: *Sony PlayStation Portable! Get it while supplies last!* "Oh, man, you think they gonna run out 'fore Christmas?"

His cousin, the bottoms of his baggy jeans hanging wet around his ankles, rolled his eyes. "C'mon. You wanted ta look at the games. Oh, hey, dudes! Look at *this*." JJ snatched up a game under a sign that screamed, *Grand Theft Auto: Liberty City Stories! New!*

Mitch punched his shoulder. "Forget it, JJ. See that 'M'? That means 'Mature.' Ya gotta be eighteen ta buy it."

"That sucks." JJ turned it over to read the back.

The other two boys sauntered along the game shelves, the intense cover graphics competing for attention. Boomer pounced. "Oh, man. This is the one I want. Forty bucks. That ain't so much."

"What's that?" Mitch looked over his shoulder.

Boomer's eyes glowed. "*Ridge Racer*. Driving simulator. Really cool, man. I played it once—"

"Lemme see that." Coming up behind them, JJ grabbed the

game, read the fine print, then waved it in his cousin's face. "Ha. Even if you *had* forty bucks, ya gotta have a PSP to use it."

"So? Told ya I'm—"

"Man comin'," Mitch hissed.

A store clerk in a rumpled white shirt hugging a paunch headed toward them, pushing past other customers until he stood in their way. "You boys buying?"

Boomer put on a smile. "Just lookin', mister."

"Well, look someplace else. Go on, git. An' keep your hands off the merchandise."

JJ shrugged. "Oh, all right. C'mon guys. Let's go."

Boomer looked at his cousin in surprise. JJ wasn't one to be pushed around. He'd expected some lip.

Out on the sidewalk, JJ headed up Clark Street at a fast clip, zigzagging around other early-evening shoppers. "Hey, wait up, JJ! Where you goin' so fast?" Mitch and Boomer scurried after him, pulling up their sweatshirt hoods and zipping their jackets, hunched against a smart wind off the lake. "What's his problem?" Mitch mumbled as JJ turned the corner at the next intersection, walking fast.

When they'd left the bright streetlights and storefronts along Clark Street, JJ turned to his two companions. "Man! He never even saw it!" Gleefully, he pulled something out of his jacket. Even in the dimmer light along the side street, Boomer could see the title: *Ridge Racer.*

"Oh, man! How'd you—?" Boomer's eyes widened. "Really? You just walked out with it?"

"Said you wanted it, didn't ya?" JJ tossed it at his cousin.

Boomer caught it. "Yeah, but . . ." He held the treasured game hungrily.

Mitch giggled nervously. "Man, oh man. You coulda got us all in big trouble back there, JJ." He laughed harder. "Ooo, JJ, you one slick dude."

JJ punched Boomer on the shoulder. "So, how 'bout a little gratitude, huh?"

Boomer frowned. "Thanks . . . I guess. 'Cept I can't play it without that PSP console."

JJ glanced down the street and suddenly pulled Boomer and Mitch into the shadows. "Well now, maybe we can fix that too."

"Whatchu mean?" Boomer craned his neck, following JJ's gaze. All he saw was a woman getting out of a car, carrying several boxes.

"Look how that lady carryin' her purse," JJ murmured.

Even in the dim streetlights along the residential street, the boys could see the woman's purse slung over one shoulder, swinging freely.

"Oh, man." Mitch's breathing got heavy. "But she's white, JJ."

"So? White women carry green money. Credit cards too."

"Hey, wait." Boomer grabbed JJ's jacket sleeve. "I don't want no trouble. I'm in enough already with my mom."

"You wanna play that video game or not, Boomer?" JJ jerked his arm away. "Now come on." He headed out of the shadows, running lightly on the snow-covered sidewalk. An adrenaline rush of excitement drowning his apprehension, Boomer followed in his cousin's wake, Mitch tight on his heels as they closed the distance to the woman walking ahead of them.

With one smooth move, JJ jerked the purse from the woman's shoulder and kept going. The jerk caused the woman to spin on the slippery sidewalk and she fell sideways, the boxes in her arms flying in all directions. "Run!" yelled JJ.

As the woman landed, she let out a cry of pain. Mitch and Boomer parted ways as if she were a traffic island they had to go around and kept running after JJ.

"Help!" the woman cried. "My ankle! . . . Somebody, help me!"

Boomer slowed and looked back. Something about that voice . . .

"Ohh . . . My ankle . . . I can't . . ."

Boomer turned. Somewhere down the street he heard JJ yelling, "Boomer! Whatchu doin'? *Come on!*"

The woman on the ground was crying, trying to get up but falling back. Desperately, Boomer looked up and down the street, hoping someone else would hear her. But no one else was out. No doors opened.

"Boomer, you *idiot!* Get outta there! . . . We're leavin', man!"

Itching to run, Boomer's feet moved like lead back to the fallen woman. She was still moaning with pain. Pulling his knit cap down low and his hood around his face, he bent slightly to get a look.

It couldn't be her. But it *was!* Half his mind screamed, *Run, idiot!* The other half said, *You can't! What if she's really hurt?*

The woman looked up. She flinched. Then she gasped, "Help me . . . please. I'm hurt. I need my cell phone. I . . . lost it when I fell. Do you see it?"

He glanced this way and that among the boxes—they were empty! But there . . . a glint in the snow. He picked it up. A silver cell phone. Without a word, he flipped it open and punched in three numbers: *9-1-1.* Then he hit Send and set it down within her reach.

And fled.

1

*T*he last time I'd stood on this sidewalk, firefighters were battling fierce flames leaping from the old church that had housed Manna House, the homeless women's shelter. Flashing red-and-blue lights had sliced through the frigid night air, heavy with smoke and the whimpers of frightened children. The blaze, started by faulty wiring and fed by a dry, brittle Christmas tree, had gutted the old church and consumed the few possessions of several dozen women and children who called the shelter "home." Bulldozers had finished the job, creating an ugly gap like a pulled tooth along the crowded row of buildings.

But today, almost two years later, crisp November sunshine brightened the narrow street in the Chicago neighborhood known as Wrigleyville. My eyes feasted on the new brick building that had risen on the same spot, its facade similar to the noble lines of the old church. A few broad steps led to a set of double oak doors, flanked by stained-glass windows on either side. At the peak of the new building, the wooden beams of a cross stretched top to bottom and side to side inside a circular stained-glass window.

"It's beautiful," I said. "Wonder what the inside is like?"

"Only one way to find out." My husband, Denny, took my arm and hustled me up the steps. A small brass plate nailed to the door said, simply, Manna House.

Instead of the dark sanctuary of the old church, a brightly lit foyer welcomed us. On the right side, a large main office with wide glass windows overlooked the foyer and room beyond; the opposite side of the foyer accommodated restrooms and an office door marked Director. Straight ahead, double doors led into a large multipurpose room in which a decent crowd filled rows of folding chairs, sat on plump couches or overstuffed chairs with bright-colored covers, or clustered around a long table with a coffee urn, a punch bowl, and plates of cookies.

"Mom! Dad! You made it!" Josh bounded over and gave us a hug. "We're just about ready to start . . . Edesa! Did you save seats for my folks?"

Josh's fiancée, Edesa Reyes, scurried over. Her thick, dark hair—longer now and caught back from her rich mahogany face into a fat ponytail at the nape of her neck—seemed to pull her broad smile from ear to ear. "Jodi! Denny! *Si*, we saved seats for you, see? Next to Avis and Peter—oh. Others are coming in." She gave each of us a warm hug. "Can't wait to give you a tour! Just don't look at *my* room. I haven't had a chance to get settled yet."

So. She'd actually given up her apartment to live on-site. I watched as Josh slipped an arm around Edesa's slim waist, turning to greet the newcomers. When did my lanky son muscle up and start looking like a grown man? He'd turned twenty-one this fall but was only in his second year at the University of Illinois, Circle Campus. Edesa, in the U.S. on a student visa from Honduras and three years his senior, had just started her master's program in public health at UIC. They'd been engaged for a year and a half—a fact that still boggled my eyeballs. But as far as we knew, no wedding plans yet.

Thank goodness. Let them get through school first—

"Sista Jodee!" A Jamaican accent hailed us from the coffee table, and Chanda George made a beeline for Denny and me, gripping a cup of hot coffee and a small plate of cookies. "Dis is so exciting! Mi can hardly believe it's happening."

Chanda had reason to be excited. After winning the Illinois Lottery Jackpot and going from single-mom-who-cleaned-houses to a multimillion-dollar bank account overnight, Chanda had gone nuts, taking her kids on exotic vacations, buying her dream house and a luxury car with leather seats—in cash—and lavishing expensive gifts on her friends. But when the women's shelter burned down, her greedy lifestyle had gotten a wake-up call: she, Chanda George, had the financial means to do major good with her unearned blessing.

"Are those cookies for me?" Denny's dimples gave him away as he helped himself to a cookie from Chanda's paper plate. "Thanks, Chanda—hey!" Denny barely caught himself from being bowled over as Chanda's two girls threw themselves at him.

"Uncle Denny!" they cried. "Where's Amanda? Ain't she home from college yet?" Cheree was leggy for ten, but eight-year-old Dia was still a Sugar Plum Fairy in my eyes: tiny, sweet, flighty, dipped in chocolate.

"Next week. She'll be home for Thanksgiving." Denny waggled his eyebrows at the girls. "Say, think you could get me some of that punch and cookies?"

The girls ran off. All three of Chanda's children, including thirteen-year-old Tom, had different fathers, none of whom had married their mother, a fact Chanda grumbled about regularly. "Dia's daddy" had come waltzing back briefly when Chanda won the lottery, and she had been sure wedding bells were in the air. But with a dozen Yada Yada Prayer Group "sisters" telling her the bum was just after her money, Chanda wised up and gave him the boot. As for Oscar Frost, the "fine" young sax player at SouledOut Community Church who Chanda had had her eye on . . . well, let's just say he treated Chanda respectfully, like an older sister. Not exactly what she'd had in mind.

Yada Yada. I glanced around the room to see how many of our prayer group had made it to the dedication of Manna House. I saw Florida Hickman serving punch at the table and even halfway across the room I could hear her chirp to the next guest in line, "How ya feel? . . . That's good, that's good."

In another corner of the room, Leslie "Stu" Stuart, who lived on the second floor of our two-flat, perched on the arm of a couch, red beret tilted to one side of her blonde head as she laughed and talked to several other Yada Yada sisters: Yo-Yo Spencer, Becky Wallace, and Estelle Williams, Stu's current housemate.

I didn't see Adele Skuggs, but the owner of Adele's Hair and Nails usually had her busiest day on Saturdays. Didn't see Delores Enriquez, either, probably for the same reason. She often had to work weekend shifts as a pediatric nurse at Cook County Hospital.

And then there were our missing sisters. Nonyameko Sisulu-Smith had been in South Africa the past year and a half, and Hoshi Takahashi had returned to Japan last summer, hoping to reunite with her estranged parents. We'd been able to keep in touch by e-mail, and the last one from Nony had Yada Yada buzzing . . .

"Avis!" I plonked into the chair beside Avis Douglass, the principal at Bethune Elementary, where I taught third grade, and the leader of our Yada Yada Prayer Group. "Did you hear any more from Nony? All she said was that they might be home before the end of the year, 'details to follow.' What does *that* mean?"

Avis shook her head. "You know as much as I do."

"Is this on?" Rev. Liz Handley, the director of Manna House, tapped on a microphone. "Good. Welcome, everyone!" The short white woman with the wire-rim glasses and cropped, salt-and-pepper hair waited a few moments as those still standing found seats. "We are delighted to see so many friends here to celebrate with us today as we dedicate Manna House II . . ." A commotion at the back of the room distracted her attention. "Come on in, folks. We're just getting started."

I turned my head. Ruth Garfield bustled in, flushed and frowsy, followed by her husband, Ben, each carrying one of their two-year-old twins. I tried to keep a straight face as Yada Yada's own Jewish *yenta* whispered, "Sorry we're late," and Yo-Yo snickered back, "So what else is new?"

Rev. Handley resumed her introduction. "I'd like to ask Peter Douglass, president of the Manna House Foundation, to say a prayer of thanksgiving as we begin."

Avis's husband rose, ever the businessman in gray slacks, navy blue blazer, and red-and-blue-striped tie. But he gave a nervous glance at his wife as he took the microphone. Avis was usually the one with the mic as one of the worship leaders at SouledOut Community Church. But Peter shut his eyes and offered heartfelt thanks to God that Manna House had "risen from the ashes, like the phoenix bird in the old tales, a symbol of renewal, resurrection, and hope to this community and its people!"

"Thank ya, *Jesus!*" Florida, who'd taken a seat behind us, leaned forward and hissed, "Now that man is not only good lookin', but that was some serious prayin'."

Avis hid a smile as Peter sat down, and Rev. Handley continued. "Before we give you the grand tour of our new facility, I'd like to introduce you to the folks who have kept the Manna House vision alive."

She called up Mabel, the office manager, a middle-aged African-American woman who got an enthusiastic round of applause. Then she introduced the board: two city pastors I didn't know, one African-American and one Latino; a social worker with reading glasses perched on her nose; and the newest board member, Peter Douglass. "Special thanks to Mr. Douglass," Rev. Handley said, "who established the Manna House Foundation after last year's fire to rebuild the shelter and—" The rest of her words were drowned out as people stood to their feet and filled the room with applause and shouts of hallelujah. Even with Chanda's major contribution, it was God's miracle that the foundation had raised enough money to rebuild.

When the noise died down, Rev. Handley read off the names of the newly formed advisory board. "Josh Baxter and Edesa Reyes, two of our volunteers. Edesa, by the way, has also taken up residence as live-in staff—"

Denny poked me and grinned. *Our kids.*

"—Estelle Williams, Precious McGill, and Rochelle Johnson, former shelter residents who have chosen to give back in this way."

The director held up her hand to forestall applause as the five made their way forward. "Because of the input of this advisory board, we have a major announcement. Victims of domestic violence who come to Manna House will now be housed off-site in private homes, a major step to provide more protection and anonymity for abused women."

The applause erupted. Beside me, Avis mopped her eyes and blew her nose. Her daughter Rochelle had run away from an abusive husband and ended up at Manna House. After the fire, Chanda had invited Rochelle and her son, Conny, to share the big house on the North Shore she'd bought with her "winnin's," and they'd stayed for nearly nine months while getting an order of protection and finalizing a divorce.

I poked Denny. "Bet that off-site idea was Rochelle's," I whispered.

"Thanks to all of you," Rev. Handley finished, "for making this day possible. And not a moment too soon. The mayor of this fine city has asked Manna House to take a busload of evacuees from Hurricane Katrina, who will be arriving from Houston tomorrow. Which means we'll have a full house for Thanksgiving dinner next week. We have a sign-up sheet on the snack table for any volunteers who'd be willing to come and serve dinner next Thursday."

The director took a breath. "Speaking of volunteers . . . " Was she looking right at me? "If you have volunteered before, or know anyone you think might be interested, please speak to me after the dedication today. And now, Pastor Rafael Kingsbury, our board chair, will say a prayer of dedication . . . "

After the brief program, I pushed my way over to Precious, who had stayed in our home for a week after the fire. "Did I hear right? Did Rev. Handley say you were a *former* shelter resident?"

"She did!" Precious beamed. "Got me a good waitress job and my own address. Sabrina doin' real well in high school too."

I had to grin. Waitressing. Not everybody's cup of tea. But Precious loved to chat up strangers and dispense her wealth of trivia, whether it was sports, astronomy, or world travel, even though her claim to travel fame had been a straight line from South Carolina to Chicago. She'd probably get big tips just because she made people laugh.

Precious lowered her voice in a conspiratorial whisper. "Don't say nothin', but I heard a rumor that Reverend Handley might just be a *former* shelter director too. She thinkin' 'bout retirin' once the shelter up an' runnin'."

Huh. I hoped she'd hang in till the new Manna House got securely on its feet. I gave Precious another quick hug and scurried to join one of the groups getting a tour through the new building. Havah Garfield, riding on her mama's hip, held out her arms to me, so I took the wavy-haired toddler to give Ruth a rest. "A ton she weighs," Ruth groaned, fanning herself with a small paper plate. "And now I have hot flashes. There ought to be medals for mothers in their fifties. What's this I hear about Nony and Mark coming back for Christmas? Has anyone heard from Hoshi? She ought to be here!"

As usual, it was hard to follow Ruth's rabbit hops from topic to topic. But the tour group was disappearing, and I wanted to see the rest of Manna House. "Let's talk about it at Yada Yada tomorrow night—your house, right? Come on, Havah. I see some toys in the next room!"

Behind the multipurpose room was a playroom, a schoolroom with computers and shelves of books, a TV room, and a small chapel. On the second floor, six medium-sized bedrooms held four bunks in each, plus showers, bathrooms, and a small central lounge. The basement boasted a well-equipped kitchen, dining room, and recreation room with Ping-Pong and foosball tables, TV and DVD player, stacks of board games, and beanbag chairs.

After the tour, people gathered in the multipurpose room for more coffee and snacks. The Garfield twins, Isaac and Havah, practiced running away from their parents and were gleefully chased by Chanda's girls and Carla Hickman, now a blossoming eleven-year-old. I lost Denny to a clump of Yada Yada husbands arguing about whether the Chicago Bears had a chance at the Super Bowl after a twenty-year slump.

"You going to sign up for Thanksgiving dinner?" I asked Florida, holding out my punch cup for a refill.

"Thanksgiving dinner? Nope. We need the family time. You?"

I rolled my eyes. "If we want to see Josh and Edesa, we better sign up. I know they'll be here." I looked around. "Where are your boys?"

Florida snorted. "Cedric's just bein' fourteen. Wants ta do his own thang on Saturday—mainly playin' video games." She shrugged. "At least I know where he is. An' you know Chris has them art classes on Saturday, down at Gallery 27." Her tone flipped from annoyed to proud.

We were all proud of Chris. Two years ago, Florida's oldest had been "tagging" walls with gang graffiti. Now he was enrolled in one of Chicago's elite art programs for youth. "*Please* let me know if he has a recital or show or whatever they call it for young artists—oh. Hi, Denny. You trying to tell me something?"

15

My husband stood there holding my coat. Florida laughed. "I wish *my* husband would come rescue me from this punch bowl. Where he at, Denny?"

I tried to sneak in a few good-byes to others, but Denny tugged my arm. "You don't have to talk to *everybody*, Jodi. You'll see half your friends at church in the morning and the other half at Yada Yada tomorrow night. Come on."

We finally slipped out the front door and started toward our car, parked around the corner by the twenty-four-hour Laundromat. The afternoon sun had dipped behind the city buildings, and the wind ripping off Lake Michigan felt more like thirty-five degrees than the actual midforties. We passed a young woman standing in the alcove of the Laundromat doorway, clutching a squalling infant wrapped in a blanket.

"Denny, wait." I turned back. The young woman in the alcove wore a sweater, but no coat. Dark hair fell over her face and down around her shoulders as she jiggled the child, who couldn't be more than three or four months old. "Um, are you okay?"

The young woman looked up. Tears streaked her face. I couldn't guess her age. She seemed maybe eighteen or twenty. On the other hand, her eyes seemed old and haggard.

The dark eyes darted to Denny, then back to me. She rattled off a string of Spanish. I didn't understand any of it, but Denny nodded. "Again. Slower."

She tried again. I heard the words *casa* and *mujeres*. "Are you looking for the women's shelter? The house for women?" Denny asked.

The girl nodded, teeth chattering. We smiled and pointed at the new building. I ran ahead, calling for Edesa as soon as I got in the door of Manna House. By the time I found her, Denny and the young mother were standing in the foyer.

"*Hola*. Welcome." Edesa's warm smile would put anyone at ease. She asked a few quick questions in Spanish, then held out her hands to the wailing baby. As Edesa cooed and rocked, the infant quieted. A moment later, Edesa ushered the girl into the private office across the hall and closed the door.

Florida had been watching from the doorway to the multipurpose room. "Huh. Them Katrina *evac-u-ees*"—she dragged out the word—"better get here fast, or it ain't gonna take long for word on the street to fill up this place."

2

I was still thinking about the girl with the baby when Denny unlocked the back door and let us into the house. I put the kettle on the stove for some hot tea, traded my shoes for slippers, and eyed the recliner in the front room.

Comfort. So easily within my reach. But that young mother . . . why was she standing out on the sidewalk in November with only a sweater? How long had she been homeless? How had she heard about Manna House? The baby was so *young.* The girl had no diaper bag, no purse, nothing. How could that be?

The teakettle whistled. Well, she was safe now. Edesa and Liz Handley and Mabel would see that both of them were well fed and tucked in tonight. *After all, that's what Manna House is all about, right, Lord?*

I heard the TV in the living room and decided to forego the recliner. Instead, I parked my mug of tea beside the computer in the dining room and booted up. I needed to e-mail Amanda and ask when she was coming home from college—and also ask if she minded doing Thanksgiving at Manna House. And maybe I'd e-mail Nonyameko and ask for details about the Sisulu-Smiths coming back to Chicago next month.

That would be *so* exciting! Yada Yada just hadn't been the same without our South African sister who "prayed Scripture" as if it were her native tongue. Had her husband, Mark, decided to return to Northwestern University after being a guest professor at the University of KwaZulu-Natal? Their school year went from January to December. Maybe Nony had realized that she could help those suffering from HIV and AIDS right here in Chicago as well as in South Africa. Like Avis's daughter Rochelle. Nony had been such a help to the Douglass family when they found out Rochelle's philandering husband had infected her with HIV. Maybe—

My in-box flooded with the standard clutter. I deleted the usual annoying spam and forwards from well-meaning friends . . . saved e-mails needing Denny's attention . . . skimmed through the latest epistle from Denny's parents who were traveling (again) through Italy, wishing *my* Iowa-bound parents would join the twenty-first century and at least get e-mail . . . when I saw it.

An e-mail from Hoshi Takahashi. *Hoshi!* Eagerly I clicked on it.

To:	Yada Yada
From:	HTakahashi@wahoo.net
Re:	Good news

Dear sisters! Thank you for praying for me these past few months. I do not have regular access to a computer here in Tokyo, but today I am in the Hibiya Library. I am encouraged to find e-mails from so many of you. Even though the visit with my family has been difficult, your prayers have not been in vain. I have only seen my parents twice since I have been home, but my aunt's heart is soft toward me—also my two younger sisters and some of my cousins.

Please keep praying for my parents, Takuya and Asuka Takahashi. I want so much for them to know the living God! But even when they allowed me to visit, they would not let me talk about Jesus. So we must pray.

I have done much thinking and praying while I have been here. For what purpose did God send me to the United States? Besides meeting Jesus and Yada Yada, that is! (VBG) As you know, God used Sara to get me involved in a Christian campus group at Northwestern. But reaching out to international students on American campuses remains large in my heart. To make short a long story, International Student Outreach has accepted my application for training starting in January. I will fly to Chicago after Christmas—

I nearly leaped out of my chair. "Hoshi's coming home!" I screeched. Wait a minute. She said *after* Christmas . . . did she know Nony and Mark might be coming home too? *Sheesh!* We had to find out when they were coming! And for how long . . . and why! It would be terrible if they missed each other.

I hit Forward on Hoshi's e-mail and typed in Nony's e-mail address. At the top of Hoshi's letter I added: "NONY! SEE BELOW. PLEASE LET US KNOW ASAP WHEN YOU'RE COMING TO

CHICAGO! DETAILS, DETAILS, DETAILS! WE WANT THEM ALL! JODI." Yeah, I knew using all caps in an e-mail was like yelling. So be it. I hit Send.

STU PULLED HER new, candy-apple-red Hyundai Accent to the curb in front of Ruth and Ben Garfield's home early the next evening. "Nice of you to get a four-door car this time, Stu," I smirked, sliding out of the backseat as she and Estelle climbed out of the front. "At least now I don't need to bring a can opener when I ride with you."

Ruth had cornered the three of us Sunday morning at SouledOut Community Church—where she and Ben often attended on Sundays, after going to services at their Messianic Jewish congregation on Saturdays—asking if some of us could come early to set out snacks for our Yada Yada prayer meeting while she and Ben gave the twins baths and got them ready for bed. Stu and Estelle, who shared the upstairs apartment of our two-flat on Lunt Street, agreed to accompany me, " . . . 'long as you two do the food thing and let me get my hands on those babies," Estelle had stipulated.

But when Ruth let us in, the twins went streaking by, naked as the day they were born, screeching and giggling, with Ben in hot pursuit yelling, "Come back here!" Sixty-something Ben was no match for the two-year-olds, who scampered through the compact living room, down the hallway, and disappeared into the kitchen at the back of the house, only to reappear a moment later from the dining room into the front hall.

Estelle and Stu pounced. "Gotcha!" Stu crowed, grabbing Isaac.

"Eek!" screeched Havah, wiggling in Estelle's firm armhold, which probably came from much practice with her own nieces and nephews back in Mississippi.

"Give Auntie Estelle some sugar," Estelle wheedled, getting a wet kiss on the nose from the giggling little girl. Then Estelle and Stu handed over the captives to their aggravated parents, who marched off toward the tub with tiny arms and legs flailing on all sides.

"Hm." Estelle headed toward the kitchen through the dining room. "Think I'll help with the food after all."

By the time the other Yada Yadas arrived, the three of us had set out teacups and a teapot wrapped in a knitted tea cozy on the dining room table, and a carafe of decaf coffee and coffee mugs, along with napkins and a plate of cinnamon star cookies from the Bagel Bakery. As the doorbell rang, Estelle disappeared to help read bedtime stories so Ruth could greet her guests and play hostess.

We had a good turnout, in spite of falling temperatures and the Thanksgiving holiday coming up. Even with Nony and Hoshi out of the country, we still had twelve sisters in our prayer group, with the addition of Becky Wallace—late twenties, white, ex-addict, ex-con—after her early parole from prison, and Estelle Williams—a fifty-something, grandmotherly African-American whom Stu took in after the Manna House fire and then invited to stay. As different as they were from each other, Becky and Estelle fit right in with the "drawer full of crazy-colored, mismatched socks" that described the Yada Yada Prayer Group.

It also helped attendance that both Delores Enriquez and Florida Hickman now had wheels, thanks to the good Lord's provision of jobs for their husbands.

"Did you look at your e-mail? Nony and Mark are coming home!"

"What? I haven't been online for a week. When? How long?"

"They didn't say. There's one from Hoshi too. Sounds like they both might be coming back to Chicago around Christmas!"

"Awriiight! We gotta have a big party."

Questions flew around Ruth's dining room table. *Are they coming back for good or just a visit? When should we have the party? Where are they going to stay?* None of us, of course, had any answers.

Avis waited until the fuss spun itself out and then simply opened with a prayer. "Lord God, we thank You that we can gather once more in Your name, to praise You for all Your mercies to us from day to day, week to week—"

"Yes, *Jesus!*" "Mm-mm." "Oh, thank You, Father . . ."

Avis left her prayer open ended, and others added their praise. "Oh, *Señor,* thank You for Manna House and that we had beds for the busload of Hurricane Katrina survivors who arrived today" . . . "Yes, yes! You're an on-time God!" . . . "Thank You for protecting our children, Lord, as they go to and from school each day" . . . "Yes, *Jes*us!" . . . "An' I wanna thank You, God, for giving Little Andy back to me an' lettin' me be his mama again. Help me to stay clean, an' help me find a bigger apartment close to my friends here—"

I opened my eyes a slit and peeked at Florida. Did she know about that? For the past two years, Becky Wallace had been subletting the two-room "apartment" on the second floor of the Hickmans' rented house. Now that Becky had regained custody of Little Andy, I could imagine the tiny space had gotten even smaller. Couldn't read Florida's face, though. Her eyes were screwed tight and she just kept nodding and murmuring, "Mm-hm."

Yo-Yo's voice broke in. "'Long as we're prayin' for the kids, God, I'm really scared they're gonna send Pete to Iraq, an' . . . an' I really don't want him to go, even though I'm glad the army's straightened him up an' he looks cool in that uniform an' every-thing . . . but he and Jerry are all the family I got . . ." Yo-Yo, who wasn't a crier, seemed to choke on the last word.

"Mm! Lord, have mercy!" Adele murmured.

We all stirred and looked up. The prayers had moved from praise to prayer requests. Avis, sensing the need to shift, went with the flow. "It sounds like Becky and Yo-Yo—and maybe others— need some time to share, and then we can pray with them. Becky? Do you want to start?"

Becky shrugged. "Well, y'all know I got me a full-time job now at UPS, an' Little Andy's in preschool. I'm grateful the way y'all have supported me while I got on my feet after prison—'specially you, Stu, for takin' me in those first six months, and the Hickmans lettin' me sublet they upstairs on the cheap. But Little Andy an' me, we on top of each other every minute, an' I'm thinkin' it'd be a good thing if we got us a bigger place."

"You sure about that, Becky?" Stu said. "Who's taking care of Little Andy right now? He's downstairs at the Hickmans', right? Times like this, you've got built-in babysitters."

Becky nodded thoughtfully. "Yeah, know what you sayin'. Still, I'm thinkin' Little Andy needs his own bedroom, a place to play, stuff like that. I've been lookin' around an' hopin' I can get somethin' in the neighborhood, so we can still be close to the Hickmans an' Baxters an' Stu."

"Come live wit' mi, Becky," Chanda said. "De kids an' me rattlin' round in dat big house since Rochelle an' Conny got dey own place. Tom still got a bunk bed in his room an' nobody usin' de guest room. Give you all de space you ever need!"

Becky grinned. "Thanks, Chanda. I 'preciate it. But I think it's time I quit lettin' you all take care of me an' Little Andy an' do what I need to do to make a home for me an' my kid."

Heads nodded in understanding. Even Florida. "But you can throw us into that prayer pot," she added. "'Cause we need to find someone else to rent Becky's place to help us make our own rent."

"Ain't never seen the righteous forsaken yet," Adele murmured. "Don't you worry, Flo. God's gonna provide for you too."

Whew. Not exactly the poetic flow of Nonyameko's "Scripture prayers," but I knew Adele's encouragement came right from Psalm 37.

"Yo-Yo?" Avis asked. "Tell us about Pete."

Yo-Yo blew her nose and stuffed the tissue back into the bib pocket of her faded denim overalls. "Ain't much to tell. He's finishing basic training at Fort Benning, then he'll be deployed somewhere. He ain't sayin' where, which makes me think . . . " Her features drew together in angry lines. "The army got that Saddam Hussein! An' the Iraqis are gonna have elections soon, ain't they? Why are we still sendin' troops over there, is what I want ta know!" She fished for her tissue again, but Ruth handed her a fresh one. "Pete drove me nuts sometimes, but he's still just a kid."

Which was true. Yo-Yo's half brothers had been her responsibility ever since I'd known her, and for several years before that.

Jerry was still in high school, but Pete had joined the army the day after he graduated last spring. Yo-Yo had been relieved at first. The army seemed just the thing for a kid who had never known a father. Not even a mother, for that matter, other than "big sis" Yo-Yo, since their mother spent most of the time strung out on drugs. But the news from Iraq these days seemed to be getting worse rather than better. Suicide bombings, Shiite versus Sunni, American troops still coming home in body bags . . .

"Best thing we can do for Pete is—" Avis started to say.

But Edesa held up her hand. "Before we pray, I want to ask prayer for Carmelita. Jodi and Denny ran into her out on the street after the dedication yesterday and brought her into the shelter. She's nineteen, single, and has a little baby, Gracie, only three months old. But Carmelita is an addict, and she has basically run out of options. We can get her into a detox program, if she'll let us. But she's afraid they'll take the baby away from her and . . . well, we don't want to scare her away. But she needs a lot of prayer."

Gracie . . . My heart tugged. I could see the squalling infant in the girl's arms, the way she quieted when Edesa held her. Why did that young woman—Carmelita—name her baby *Gracie*? Was it a family name?

Or a cry for mercy?

3

*T*hanks for the ride, Stu."
I unlocked our back door and stepped into the kitchen as Stu and Estelle climbed the outside stairs to their second-floor apartment. Even though Willie Wonka had been gone the last year and a half, I still half expected to hear the click of the old dog's nails on the tile and feel his cold nose nuzzling my hand when I came in the house. But the kitchen was dark, silent, and empty. Even the TV blathering away in the living room seemed to come from another dimension.

Empty nest. Did it have to happen so suddenly? First Wonka died after growing up with the kids, like a "blankie" that finally lost the last of its comforting, silky binding. Then Josh got an apartment with a couple of roommates near UIC's Chicago campus. And now Amanda was three hours away at the University of Illinois in Champaign-Urbana.

Denny and I simply didn't make enough hubbub to fill the empty spaces. I sighed and flipped on the kitchen light—

"SURPRISE!"

My keys flew out of my hand, bounced off a cupboard, and landed in the sink. Two heads poked into sight from either side of the doorway leading into the dining room, grinning like puppets.

"Amanda!" I screeched. "When did . . . why didn't you *tell* me you were coming home tonight!" *And who is this total stranger in our house?* I wanted to add. *Male.*

Amanda bopped into the kitchen and gave me a big hug. Her thick, butterscotch-colored hair was caught at the back of her head with an oversize clip, tendrils dangling carelessly front and sides. "Had to catch a ride when I could get one, Mom. And this is Neil. You said I could bring a friend home from school for Thanksgiving, remember?"

Well, yes. But I'd imagined her roommate, or a darling international student from Norway or Kenya. Not this overgrown football player with a neck as thick as Denny's thigh. "Hey there," he said, flipping his finger off his forehead as if he were tipping a hat.

Denny showed up in the kitchen doorway, grinning so wide you could probably lose a quarter inside his dimples. "She called after you left for Yada Yada. She wanted to surprise you."

Amanda giggled. "Yeah. We scared her so bad, she won't get hiccups for the next ten years."

Neil, we learned over popcorn and soft drinks, was at U of I on a football scholarship from Tallahassee and didn't have the bucks to go home for Thanksgiving. When he found out that Amanda's dad was a high school athletic director, he'd practically invited himself home with her, probably imagining nonstop TV football over Thanksgiving. Amanda, who was a pushover for strays of all species, had agreed to let him tag along.

At least Josh's bed was available. "But I didn't realize she had *all week* for Thanksgiving vacation," I hissed to Denny behind our bedroom door when we'd said goodnight to Amanda and her guest. "*We've* still got three more days of school . . . which leaves them alone at the house all day."

"Hm." Denny crawled into bed and turned on his reading light.

"What about our rule about not being alone in the house with the opposite sex?"

Denny sighed. "Yeah. But we can't exactly kick them out from eight to five, can we? She's eighteen now, Jodi. We have to trust our daughter."

"*Humph.*" I crawled into bed. "I trust Amanda. Can't say the same for Mr. Tallahassee."

BOTH COLLEGE STUDENTS were still hibernating in their respective dens when Denny and I left the house the next morning. "I know!" I told Denny, who'd offered to drop me off at Bethune Elementary on his way to West Rogers High. "If Amanda has the whole week for Thanksgiving, Josh probably does too. They're both U of I campuses. Where's the cell? I'll call and see if he can drop in today to see his sister."

Denny surrendered the cell phone without rolling his eyes, but I could tell he wanted to. I got Josh on the third ring. "Hi, hon. Hope I didn't wake you . . . . Oh. Okay . . . No, just wanted to tell you Amanda's home. Talk to you later." I handed the phone back to Denny.

"What?" He was grinning at me.

"Said he was on his way to his eight o'clock class." I shrugged.

31

"Guess UIC isn't on break yet. Oh, well." I'd just have to leave the whole thing to God. But I *was* going to talk to Amanda about the awkward situation.

I scurried past the school office without stopping, wanting to slip into my classroom and enjoy the next thirty minutes of peace before I had to go out on the playground and round up my third graders. I dumped the bag of items I'd brought from home for our unit on renewable/nonrenewable sources of energy and shed my coat. With an eye on the clock, I started my Monday routine— praying for each of the kids in my class by name as I walked up and down the rows of desks.

"Lord, show me how to keep loving on Portia. She always comes back to school after a weekend looking like a scared rabbit . . . Thank You, God, that Bernie has settled down and is showing some interest in science . . . Hm, bless the twins, Lord, Selena and Saleem. Give me more understanding of the culture they're coming from . . . But it's patience I need for Randy, Lord. What *is* it with his constant chatter? . . . Bless sweet Sophia, Lord. She's got such a kind heart. Protect her heart, Lord; don't let it get calloused . . ."

The bell rang just as I finished the prayers for my students, sending the day into its usual nonstop orbit—taking attendance, collecting take-home folders, reciting the Pledge of Allegiance led by a fifth grader over the school intercom, squashing skirmishes before they escalated into actual fights, trying to supervise the language arts worksheet on synonyms while bringing different reading groups to the Story Rug . . .

Lunch break for third and fourth grade arrived too soon in terms of work *not* accomplished that morning, and not soon enough in terms of my energy level. At least I wasn't on lunchroom supervision. I took the opportunity to stop by the school office and peek in on Avis. "You got a minute?"

Trim and professional in a black pantsuit with a red, silky blouse, Avis looked up from the stack of papers she was signing and waved me in. "What's up?"

I closed the door. "Nothing school related. What are you making for Thanksgiving dinner at Manna House? I saw your name on the list."

She made a face. "Macaroni and cheese, what else? I *know* they'll have turkey. But I don't trust anyone else to make mac 'n cheese the way my family likes it. Besides . . . " She let slip an impish grin. "It's the only thing I know how to make without a recipe. You?"

"Pies, I guess. Hope I'm not the only one. Four's my limit before going crazy."

"Great. Is that it?" She indicated the stack of papers she'd been working on.

"Sorry. I'm going." I opened the door. "Oh, just wanted to tell you Amanda's home, brought a friend from U of I. He's from Tallahassee. I don't like him, and for the life of me I can't give you a good reason."

Avis laughed. "Mm. Been there. Talk to you later."

I HUSTLED HOME after school, the rod in my left leg aching with the dipping temperatures. That rod, and needing to take extra vitamins to keep my immune system well padded because of my missing spleen, were the only side effects I still experienced from the car accident I'd had a few years ago. But the ache in my heart for the mother of the teenager I'd killed was still fresh every time I thought about the startling sequence of events that had put his little brother in my classroom the next school year. Hakim had worked his way into my heart—much to his mother's fury—and I often wondered where he was and how he was doing. *By now Hakim would be*—I mentally counted years as I dragged up our front steps and took the mail out of the box—*in sixth grade. Ouch. Almost a teenager.* I sent up an extra prayer. Middle school could be tough even without the trauma he'd faced after losing his older brother.

"Amanda?" I called from the front hall as I let myself in. No answer. The house was empty. A note on the dining room table said: *Went downtown to show Neil around. Josh called. Coming for supper.*

Hey. That would be nice. Extra nice that Josh thought of it himself without me asking. I pulled out some chicken pieces from the freezer . . . and had crusty, oven-baked chicken in the oven by the time Amanda and Neil came in, red-nosed and hungry. Josh and Denny arrived within minutes of each other and the house was suddenly, gloriously full of everyone talking at once.

I grinned at Denny as we gathered around the dining room table. This was more like it. The kids home, a guest at our table . . . who stuck a fork in a piece of chicken on the platter in front of him and hefted it onto his plate. "Looks good, Mrs. Baxter."

"Yes it does," Denny said smoothly, and added, "but let's take a moment to give thanks." He held out his hands to Josh on one side of him and a puzzled Neil on the other, and we all joined hands and bowed heads as Denny gave a short prayer of thanks. Good thing *he* prayed. I would have been tempted to pray for all the missionaries and trouble spots around the world and keep Mr. Tallahassee waiting.

But the awkwardness passed and Amanda and Neil chatted back and forth about riding the el train (a first for Neil), seeing the city from the top of Sears Tower, and wandering around the artsy shops along Rush Street. "We might take in one of the museums tomorrow—do you know how many years it's been since I've been to the Museum of Natural History? And I *live* in Chicago!" she said, waving her fork. "But Wednesday I'm going to be working with some of the girls at church, choreographing a candle-lighting dance for the first Sunday of Advent. Neil's going to have to entertain himself."

"Whoa." Denny's eyebrows went up. "Is it Advent already? We haven't even had Thanksgiving!"

"Da-ad. It's *always* the first Sunday after Thanksgiving. Well, usually. Pastor Clark called me and asked if I'd be willing to recreate the candle dance I did at Uptown a few years ago."

"So. Josh," said Neil, his mouth full of mashed potatoes. "What's your major?"

"International Studies."

"Really? Huh." Neil digested that for a whole nanosecond. "Who ya think's gonna go to the Rose Bowl this year?"

4

I wasn't sure I was going to survive a whole week with the football player from Tallahassee. "Take it easy, Jodi," Denny soothed when I grumbled about his rudeness at the table. "Maybe God has a reason for bringing him to our home."

I glared at him as I pulled on my warm pajamas. "Yeah, well, that reason better not have anything to do with our daughter."

Denny laughed. "I doubt it. A week with Super Jock underfoot ought to get on Amanda's nerves too."

A giggle threatened to undo my crankiness. "Hm. Dunno about that. You've been underfoot for twenty-three years and we still—"

"Hey!" Denny swatted my shoulder. "I can hold up my end of a conversation."

"Yeah, and you've got cute dimples going for you too." I pinched his cheek like an obnoxious great-aunt.

"Ha. So it's a pinching free-for-all, is it?" Denny made a grab for my pajama-clad bottom, but I squealed and leaped across the bed to the far side—only to realize he'd darted around the end of the bed and cornered me.

Squealing like a stuck pig, I scrambled back across the bed just out of his reach, rumpling our wedding-ring quilt into messy lumps. I grabbed a pillow and held it for protection. "I give! I give! No pinching!"

Sudden banging on our bedroom door stopped us both in mid-laughter. "Dad! Mom! What's going on in there?"

We both clamped hands over our mouths. Denny waited a beat, then opened the door a crack. "Playing. None of your business."

"Well, it's embarrassing," Amanda hissed through the crack. "Neil and I can hear you clear in the living room!" Her footsteps tromped back down the hall.

I collapsed on the bed, muffling my giggles with a pillow. Denny waggled his eyebrows at me. "Guess we better behave," he growled in a loud whisper. "Don't want to give our guest any ideas."

IT SNOWED WEDNESDAY, our first snow of the season. "Yeaaa!" yelled my students, flying out the door when the last bell rang, jackets askew and backpacks bumping. The weatherman had only predicted an inch, but it covered the concrete city prettily, muffling my footsteps as I walked home on the unshoveled walks. Might as well enjoy it now. It would probably be gone tomorrow.

Four wonderful vacation days stretched out before me. *Amanda's home . . . Thanksgiving dinner will be a cinch, since all I have to do is make a few pies . . . maybe we'll hear from the Sisulu-Smiths and can start planning for our Yada Yada reunion . . .*

Neil was alone in our living room, watching a game show on TV. He looked up when I came in the front door. "You guys don't get ESPN?"

"Sorry. We don't have cable." *Be sweet, Jodi.* "Is Amanda here?"

He shook his head, eyes glued to the TV. "Nah. She's over at your church, doing that . . . whatever she's doing."

"You decided not to go along? There are some funky shops along Howard Street." I felt double-minded, half irritated that he let her walk by herself all the way to Howard Street, half glad they weren't together every minute.

"Yeah, she asked. But it's a blizzard out there." He shivered. "No thanks."

Blizzard. Mr. Tallahassee had no idea.

I left our guest to the TV and headed for the kitchen. I had pies to make. Tying on an apron, I hauled out the canister of flour, can of shortening, box of salt, and measuring spoons. "So, Wonka, what shall I make first? Pumpkin? Apple?" I stopped myself. The talking-to-Willie-Wonka-while-I-cooked habit was hard to break.

Hm. Maybe it's time to get Amanda a new dog. I smiled as I mixed four batches of pie dough, cutting the shortening into the flour until it looked like floury peas, then sprinkling ice water over the mixture just until it clung together. *A puppy for Christmas—what fun!*

Just as quickly, I nixed that idea. Amanda would be living in a dorm for the next four years, except for summers. Hardly the time to get her a pet.

Neil wandered into the kitchen. "Whatcha making? Homemade pies? Cool." He parked himself on the kitchen stool. He weighed at least two hundred pounds, all of it muscle. I wasn't sure our wimpy stool was going to survive. *Might as well make the best of it.* I handed him a bowl of apples and a peeler. "Mind helping? Just peel the skin off those apples."

"Oh. Uh, sure." He applied himself to the task, frowning in concentration, tip of his tongue sticking out the side of his mouth. "So what else is on the menu for Thanksgiving dinner? Will Josh and his fiancée be here too? Broncos are playing the Cowboys in Dallas. Oughta be a tight game. Hoo! Hoo!" He waved the peeler and grinned.

I stopped rolling out piecrusts and stared at our guest. Hadn't anyone told him? "Um, Neil, we're not having Thanksgiving dinner here. We're taking these pies to the Manna House women's shelter—Josh and Edesa are volunteers there. So our family signed up to help serve Thanksgiving dinner. But don't worry," I hastened to add, "it ought to be a big spread, lots of good food."

He gaped at me as my words slowly registered. "A women's shelter? Like, you mean, bums off the street, except broads?"

Count to ten, Jodi. Slowly . . . one . . . two . . . three . . .

"Actually, right now most of the Manna House *residents* are evacuees from New Orleans, after Hurricane Katrina. They're definitely homeless." I felt heat rising in my face. "Could be you, or me, you know, if we lived in New Orleans."

"Huh! Not me." Neil tackled another apple. "I would've got out of there before that storm hit. All the smart people did." Then he frowned and looked up. "Hey. We gonna be back here by three? The game starts at three-fifteen!"

As FAR AS I was concerned, Neil-from-Tallahassee could just stay home and watch his stupid football game. Denny said he was sure Manna House would have the game on in the TV room. But God and I had a silent scuffle all the way down to the Wrigleyville neighborhood the next day in the minivan.

Jesus, I know You told us to love our enemies, but does that include extremely annoying people?

Never said it would be easy, Jodi.

Yeah, but we've got four days to go! I'm afraid I'm gonna say something I regret—or pop him one.

Have you asked Me for My grace, Jodi? And by the way, Denny was right. I brought Neil to your home for a purpose. Sow the seeds, Jodi. Sow the seeds.

I let out a long sigh.

Dinner was scheduled for one o'clock, but we pulled into a parking space around the corner from Manna House about noon. With each of us carrying a pie—two apple and two pumpkin—we trundled down the stairwell to the side door on the lower level. The outside door was locked, but after a few moments, Precious answered the shrill doorbell.

"Baxters! Whatchu comin' in the basement door for—oh! Pies. Just take 'em on over there to the dessert table . . . *Amanda!*" A squeal and a hug. "Girl, when did you get home from school? Here—let me take that pie . . . *Sabrina!* Look who's here!" Precious lowered her voice but not her grin. "She been hopin' you'd come."

Sabrina, looking smart and skinny in layered clingy tops with her midriff showing, waved shyly from the door of the rec room. Amanda scooted in that direction, where a handful of noisy kids were playing Ping-Pong and foosball, leaving Neil with us. But after depositing his pie, he followed. A quick peek into the rec room a few minutes later assured me all was well: Neil was parked in front of the TV in the corner.

"What can we do to help?" I asked Precious. A bevy of assorted women were already in the kitchen, chattering, banging pots and pans, loading up baskets of rolls, and setting out aluminum pans over hot-water warmers on the serving table. "Some of the new residents?"

Precious rolled her eyes. "Yes, ma'am. An' the stories they got to tell! Lord Jesus, have mercy! Picked off rooftops, left in a stadium without enough food an' water, bused here an' there, never knowing where they gonna sleep next, with just the clothes on they backs. Bad as it can be here in Chicago, I ain't *never* goin' back to live in no hurricane alley . . . Denny! Find Peter Douglass—he's around here somewhere. We gonna need some more tables. Jodi, take these tablecloths and cover what we already got. We got some candle centerpieces to make 'em pretty-like. But don't light them candles! Uh-uh. No way."

The "tablecloths" were white plastic, but the tables looked festive with the pillar candles sitting in a wreath of fake fall leaves. Food kept arriving, along with familiar faces. By the time one o'clock rolled around, the serving tables were crowded with platters of sliced turkey, bowls of mashed potatoes, gravy, corn bread dressing, sliced ham, Avis's macaroni and cheese, Chanda's big pot of Jamaican rice and peas, and another of sautéed cabbage and carrots. Stu and Estelle had brought more desserts—cranberry nut bread and apple crisp—and Florida had sent along a couple of sweet potato pies.

The dining room filled up as the tempting aromas drew people downstairs from the main level, both residents and guests. The Katrina evacuees were an assorted bunch, mostly black, a few white, a few Cajun, all women, most with young children. Families with husbands or male teenagers, I'd been told, were being sheltered in other facilities.

But I hadn't yet seen either Josh or Edesa, even though Precious told me they were around . . . strange. I hustled up the stairs to the all-purpose room as the last stragglers were coming down. Edesa was standing near the double doors leading into the foyer talking to Liz Handley, jiggling a baby on her shoulder.

" . . . go on downstairs, Edesa," Rev. Handley was saying as I came up. "I'll wait here for Josh and keep an eye out for any late guests. I'm sure he'll find her."

"No, no, Reverend Liz. You are the hostess for this Thanksgiving Day. Gracie and I can wait—oh. *Hola*, Jodi."

"What's going on?" I asked.

Edesa shrugged. "Carmelita went out a few hours ago to buy some diapers for the baby, asked if I would take care of her till she got back." She nuzzled the baby and smiled. "Who could say no? *La bebé es tan preciosa.*" The dark-eyed baby waved a fist and grabbed a lock of Edesa's hair, cooing happily. But Edesa's frown returned. "But it's been three hours, and she is still not back. Josh went out to look for her—oh!"

The front door opened, and Josh came in . . . alone.

THANKSGIVING DINNER AT Manna House was a merry affair, in spite of the dire circumstances that had brought most of the current residents. Neil seemed reluctant to leave the TV—another

Thanksgiving Day game was already in play—but he dutifully trailed Amanda to the table, with several adoring little boys hanging on his arms who had discovered he played *college football.* Laughter, tales of Thanksgiving dinners past, and hauling little ones out from under the tables were punctuated by second and third trips to the food tables.

We did more than eat. As paper plates were cleared and coffee was perking to go with the desserts—I noticed a run on Florida's sweet potato pies—Rev. Handley encouraged people to share their thanksgivings on this day. I watched Neil as women whose lives had been totally disrupted by the recent hurricane gave thanks to God.

" . . . that all my children are with me today, alive and safe."

"I'm thankful to be at Manna House. It's the nicest place we've stayed yet."

"I'm just thankful to be *alive*. Some of my neighbors didn't make it."

Even little voices piped up. "I got to ride in a helicopter!" . . . "I'm thankful for my mommy. She held onta me when the big wind came." . . . "A nice lady in Houston gave me this teddy bear."

Three o'clock came and went and Neil was still at the table.

But by the time the tables had been cleared, trash bags taken out to the alley bins, leftovers bagged, and good-byes said, Carmelita had still not returned.

5

I worried all the way home. "Shouldn't they call the police? I mean, a missing mother . . ."

"Edesa said they don't want to do that yet," Amanda piped up from the second seat. "The police would take the baby to DCFS, and she'll end up who-knows-where in a foster home."

"But isn't that what foster homes are for? Maybe it would be a good thing. More stability than little Gracie has now."

"I think they're trying to buy a little time," Denny said. "Josh said Edesa would really like to help Carmelita and doesn't want to give up yet."

But if Carmelita has abandoned her baby . . .

I stared out the passenger-side window at the last vestiges of yesterday's snow melting off store awnings and gathering into puddles on the sidewalks and in the street. *Okay, Lord, I realize I'm stewing instead of praying. Please bring Carmelita back to Manna House. That baby needs her mother. Wherever she is, Lord, keep her safe. Give Manna House wisdom about what to do . . .*

We pulled into our garage about four-thirty. Neil had been quiet on the way home. "Sorry you missed your game," I said, feeling a twinge of compassion for the oversize freshman, still just a kid, miles from home, who was at the mercy of our family schedule.

"It's okay. Mind if I catch the second half?"

Denny grinned as he unlocked the back door. "My plan exactly."

THE PHONE RANG later that evening just as we settled down to a big bowl of popcorn, soft drinks, and the latest card game making the rounds of the dorms at U of I. I was tickled when Amanda said she'd teach us how to play Phase 10. It'd been a long time since we'd played games as a family—though it wasn't exactly "family" with Neil shuffling cards and making up the fourth player.

Huh, I thought, jumping up for the phone. *Would Josh have come home to spend the holidays if we hadn't given away his bedroom all week?*

"Mom?" Josh's voice sang in my ear, as if he knew I'd been thinking about him. "Just wanted to let you guys know that Carmelita showed up about an hour ago."

"Josh! That's wonderful." I turned and gave a thumbs-up to the others at the dining room table. "Is she okay?"

"Mm. Not really. She's high on something. But at least she came back. Edesa's going to take care of the baby until she sobers up."

"I thought Manna House kicked people out if they used drugs."

For two seconds, all I heard was silence on the other end. Then,

"Yeah. That's the rule. But there's Gracie to think of. Reverend Handley is going to help Carmelita enroll in a detox program tomorrow. Maybe they'll find one that'll take both Carmelita and the baby."

"Okay, hon. Thanks for letting us know. We'll keep praying for her and the baby." I hung up the phone and went back to the table. "Guess you all heard that Carmelita came back. High on something." I picked up my hand of cards—then laid them down again. "I said we'd pray for her and the baby. Let's do it now, okay?"

I hesitated a nanosecond, and then held out my hands to Amanda and Neil on either side of me. Neil looked bewildered but saw that the rest of us were joining hands and did likewise. I closed my eyes to help me focus on our prayers, not on what our guest might be thinking.

IT SNOWED AGAIN the next day—mere flurries—but Amanda begged her dad to take us all to the Walker Bros. Pancake House in Wilmette. "And we gotta do Gulliver's tomorrow night. I told Neil about Chicago's great pizza." Both restaurants were family favorites—not just for the great food, but for the museum quality and quantity of the stained glass at Walker Bros., and the statuary and old-fashioned "gas" lamps at Gulliver's.

"Hey. How deep do you think my pockets are?" Denny protested. "Tell you what. I'll treat for Walker Bros.; you and Neil can go out to Gulliver's on your own dime."

I winced. He was practically sending them on a *date*. But I had to laugh when I later discovered that Amanda invited the teen girls she was working with on the Advent candle dance to go with them to Gulliver's after their practice Saturday afternoon.

Poor Neil.

Of course, that meant Denny and I were without a car on a Saturday night. We'd both put in several hours the past two days grading papers or, in Denny's case, ironing out glitches in West Rogers High's soccer and baseball schedules for spring. But I used the time to get out our box of Christmas decorations and set up the Advent candle wreath we used during the four weeks leading up to Christmas Day.

Denny came back from a sunset run along the lake and grinned when he saw the box of Christmas decorations on the dining room table. He pulled out a DVD from his sweatshirt pocket. "Then I guess you won't mind me getting a jump-start on the holidays with this." He waggled the DVD in my face—the 1951 version of *A Christmas Carol* with Alastair Sim as Scrooge. "My favorite. I waited too long last year, and it was never in stock."

NEIL SEEMED TONGUE-TIED when we arrived at SouledOut Community Church the next morning. Whether it was the fact that the church was just a large storefront in the new Howard Street Mall—though roomy and bright, with a bank of windows facing the mall and colorful walls—or whether it was our multi-hued congregation, I couldn't tell. Josh and Edesa came in soon after us, walking from the Howard Street el station. Since they had gotten engaged, they often alternated Sundays between SouledOut and Edesa's congregation, *Iglesia del Espirito Santo,* on the west side. Sometimes they each attended their own churches, especially since Josh often helped with SouledOut's youth outreach.

"Good to see you both," I murmured, giving them each a hug. "I enjoyed Thanksgiving at Manna House, but I kind of missed just having some family time with the two of you—not to mention that we had no turkey leftovers this year." I rolled my eyes to keep it light.

"Anytime you want turkey leftovers, Mom, just stick a bird in the oven and I'll—oh. Hey there, Neil." Josh shook Neil's hand, then swiveled his head. "Is Amanda dancing this morning? Edesa wouldn't let us miss it."

"Not sure. She's been teaching a group of young teen girls to do the dance . . . guess we'll see. Want to sit with us?"

"*Si.*" Edesa beamed. "I want to see *mi hermana* dance."

Mi hermana. "My sister." Amanda had always been crazy about Edesa, ever since Edesa had tutored her in freshman Spanish. She was going to love having Edesa as a "big sister." *Huh. Sister.* That's what we called each other in Yada Yada. As much as I loved Edesa, I wasn't sure I wanted to exchange the relationship of being "sister" for *mother-in-law.*

Instead of the usual call to worship by the worship leader, someone flicked the lights and then turned them off to quiet the congregation, and the last ones standing found seats. And instead of the band launching into the usual rousing praise song, Oscar Frost picked up his saxophone and began a slow rendition of the Advent hymn "O Come, O Come, Emmanuel."

A small table at the front held a large evergreen wreath lying flat. Embedded in the greenery were three purple pillar candles and one pink one. In the middle stood a white pillar candle. One of the African-American teenagers—she looked about fourteen, but the praise team had already used her for some get-down gospel solos—stood off to the side and sang majestically:

O come, O come, Emmanuel,
And ransom captive Israel . . .

At the same time, eight teenage girls stepped in time to the music down the two aisles that divided the congregation—four down each aisle—a mix of skin colors and body types, from slender to chunky, tall and short. Each one carried a lit taper candle. They were dressed alike, in black silky skirts that hung to midcalf, matching silky white blouses, black tights, and black ballet slippers. Disappointed, I realized Amanda was not one of the eight girls. But of course it had to be that way; she was going back to school this afternoon. *Bless her, Father, for being willing to pass the torch.*

. . . That mourns in lonely exile here . . .

The eight girls fanned out as they reached the front, hiding their bowed faces in the crook of one arm.

. . . Until the Son of God appears . . .

The girls now held their candles out in front of them, faces lifting up with expectant joy.

Rejoice! Rejoice!—

Many in the congregation, as if on cue, joined in on the refrain, helping to swell the music. The dancers reached upward with their lighted candles and moved in a lovely circle around the table with the Advent wreath.

—*Emmanuel*
Shall come to thee, O Israel!

Two of the dancers moved to the table and tipped their candles toward one of the purple pillars, lighting the first candle. And as the last notes of the saxophone drifted away, all the girls blew out their tapers.

Someone down the row was blowing his nose. I peeked around Denny.

It was Neil.

THE VANLOAD OF college students picked up Amanda and Neil from SouledOut even before the worship service was over. Denny and I slipped out of the service with them and got their duffel bags from the back of our minivan, transferred them to the other car, and said our good-byes. Josh and Edesa slipped out too.

"Bye, big brother." Amanda gave Josh a hug. "Don't do anything I wouldn't do."

"Ha. That gives me a lot of leeway, squirt." He turned to Neil and shook hands. "Good luck on the gridiron."

Neil nodded. He shook our hands. "Thanks, Mr. and Mrs. Baxter. Really appreciate you putting me up for Thanksgiving." He waved and climbed into the van.

"Call when you get there," I told Amanda as I hugged her. "Just want to know you got back safely."

"Don't worry, Mom. See you in a few weeks!" Amanda finished her round of hugs and popped into the car. The side door slid closed and the van drove out of the shopping center and turned down Howard Street toward Sheridan Road.

The four of us went back inside SouledOut. Worship was still going on. But I dreaded going back to our empty house. Maybe Josh and Edesa could come by for lunch . . . but eventually I knew they'd leave too. I felt my throat tighten and tears threatened to muddy my makeup.

Did my parents blubber like this when I went back to school after holidays? My two brothers had already left home; I was the baby of the family and tired of having strict parents looking over my shoulder. I couldn't wait to fly out of the nest. I knew my parents missed me; they always said so. But I'd never really thought of how "missing" actually *felt*—like one's own soul had flown away.

So when we got Amanda's call later that afternoon, I wanted to clutch the phone and hold it to my heart. But—*duh, Jodi, grow up!*—I pushed the speakerphone button so both Denny and I could hear.

"Yep, trip went fine, no snow down here at all . . . but it was kinda interesting to hear Neil talk about the week at our house."

"He *talked*?" Denny said. I punched his shoulder.

"Yeah. He said that Thanksgiving at his house was always just a lot of eating and football games on TV. But he can't remember his family ever actually giving thanks to God for anything—saying it aloud, he meant. He was really touched—yeah, that's the word he used: 'touched'—when the hurricane evacuees all had something to give thanks for, even the little kids . . . Oh, and he said that was the first time he'd gone to church in a long time too. I guess the Advent dance and the song about expecting the Son of God to come, and those verses Pastor Cobbs preached on from the Old Testament, really made him think—though he called having church in a shopping center a little weird."

My heart softened toward the young man from Tallahassee. God had told me to *"sow the seeds"* . . . but I realized God had used the whole fabric of our lives to touch Neil's heart. Amanda's invitation to come home with her, spending Thanksgiving Day at a shelter full of destitute women and children, holding hands around our table as we prayed for Carmelita, playing games and laughing, thanking God for our food at Walker Bros. Pancake House, taking him to church, sharing the Word of God through song and dance and the Word—all woven together in a way we probably took for granted.

Huh. I also realized how easily I could have ruined the gentle tapestry God was weaving. *Thanks, God, for keeping me from shooting off my big mouth.*

"So." Denny cleared his throat. "You two pretty good friends?" He gave me a look that said, *Might as well ask instead of guess.*

Amanda hooted on the other end of the phone. "Are you kidding? I am so relieved to have him off my hands, I could dance all over the campus! Longest Thanksgiving vacation of my whole life."

I could hardly wait to end the call so I could laugh aloud. *She* was relieved? That made two of us!

6

Crrr-raaaack-ba-boom!

A clap of thunder so loud it sounded as if a chain saw was ripping the school apart was equaled only by the screams of a dozen of my third graders, who dove under their desks. "Class, class, it's all right; it's only thunder," I tried to soothe. But another *crrr-aaaack!* and a streak of lightning outside our classroom window drowned out my words.

I glanced at the thermometer mounted just outside the window. Sixty degrees. *Sheesh.* What weird weather we were having. Below freezing and our first snow last week; now, the first school day after the Thanksgiving holiday, balmy as spring—what my mom used to call "Indian summer" after the first frost. But the mild temperatures had also cooked up a major thunderstorm, which was now slashing rain against the windows and turning the sky a creepy green.

By the time the last bell rang, the rain had slackened to a mere drizzle, but I was still pretty soaked by the time I got home, and the temperature was falling again. Shivering, I stripped off my wet clothes, hopped in the shower, warmed myself up with Denny's robe and a cup of hot tea, and booted up the computer to check e-mail.

Whoa! Eighty new messages. Huh. You'd think I would have stayed current during the holidays, but with Amanda home, a guest in the house, and all that extra cooking, I just never got around to it.

I scrolled through the e-mails. *Spam . . . Weekly calendar from SouledOut . . . This is cute—pass it on* (from one of my college class-mates who never wrote a personal note but jammed my in-box with "Fwd. Fwd. Fwds") . . . *More spam—*

Hey! One from Nony. Sent two days ago. I clicked it open . . .

To: Yada Yada
From: BlessedRU@online.net
Subject: Re: Details! Details!

We are so excited, dear Yada Yada sisters, to see you soon! The end of the boys' school term is 2 December, but Mark very much wants to stay for the National Day of Reconciliation, which is 16 December. This year is especially momentous, as it is the tenth anniversary of the establishment of the Truth and Reconciliation Commission after the end of apartheid. There will be speeches, concerts . . . an important public holiday in South Africa.

So we will be arriving in Chicago sometime the week right after Christmas. I will let you know details as soon as our plans are finalized. This only gives us three weeks to sell our house in

Evanston and get back in time for the new school year, which
starts 18 January, but—

My heart clutched. *"Sell our house . . . get back . . . "* Nony and
Mark must have decided to make the move to KwaZulu-Natal
permanent! Had I missed something? Wasn't Mark on *sabbatical*
from Northwestern University? Didn't that mean he was supposed
to come back?

I stared at the computer screen, my emotions churning. Okay.
Sure. Part of the reason they'd gone to South Africa was to explore
whether to follow Nony's heart and relocate long term. Mark had
accepted a position as guest lecturer in the history department at
the University of KwaZulu-Natal. Emphasis on *guest*. Nony had
put feet to her passion and gotten involved with HIV/AIDS
classes in schools. But frankly, I'd been hoping, praying—okay,
assuming—they'd come back to the States after a year or two.
After all, Mark and the boys were as American as we were!

Jodi, Jodi. The Holy Spirit interrupted my inner rant. *What happened to, "Not my will but Thy will be done"?*

I know, Lord, but—

*That goes for your love for Nony and her family too. I have them in
the palm of My hand. But you must open yours and hold them loosely,
My daughter.*

I squeezed my eyes shut, resisting the urge to stop up my inner
ears. *But I miss Nony so much.*

I know. You will see her soon. Be glad! Celebrate!

I opened my eyes. Right. That's what we needed to do when
Nony arrived—celebrate! Party! Hoshi would be back, too,
hopefully.

Okay, Lord, we're going to enjoy them while we can. And . . . thank You for bringing this beautiful sister into my life. What a gift she has been to me and to all the Yada Yadas! But You're right—she's a gift, not a possession. Nony belongs to You.

I was just about ready to shut down the computer and start supper for Denny and me (which these days often meant warming up leftovers from the night before) when a new e-mail went *ping!*—and popped into my in-box.

From Becky Wallace. She hardly ever sent e-mails. Curious, I opened it.

To: Yada Yada
From: Boundbygrace@wahoo.com
Subject: need boxes!

hey, sisters, i think i found an apartment that's going to work for me and little andy. i can move in dec 17 but i need boxes. lots of boxes. i have more stuff now than i did when i moved in here, ha ha. you can bring them to yy on sunday, we're meeting here, at florida's house i mean. thanks! becky

Huh. Somebody needed to show that girl what the Shift key was for.

SOME INDIAN SUMMER. It lasted all of one soggy day, and then all hat rain froze, leaving the side streets, sidewalks, and alleys slick ith ice. Not to mention tree branches and iron fences, sparkling like exquisite ice sculptures under the streetlights. The ice on the ground was deceptive, melting in places during the day, then refreezing thin and clear at night like a newly waxed floor.

All of which made lugging home the boxes that I'd collected at school a bit tricky. Taking baby steps along the sidewalks, walking on crunchy patches of grass where I could, it took me twice as long to get home as it normally did. "Should've just stuffed these boxes in Avis's car and let *her* bring them to Becky on Sunday," I muttered to the empty house as I finally made it, still upright, inside our front door and kicked the boxes into the foyer ahead of me.

Denny—whose motto seemed to be, "If one is good, more must be better!"—arrived home with four more boxes, neatly nestled one inside the other. "Thought Becky could use these. They've been sitting around the athletic department for a week."

I surveyed the stacks of boxes in our dining room. Why did I even bother bringing boxes home before Friday? Now they'd be sitting around *our* house all week.

"Tell you what," Denny said, gamely pushing boxes into a corner so we could eat our leftover fettuccine at the dining room table. "Oscar Frost offered to pick me up at school one of these Thursday nights and do the driving down to the JDC. You can take *me* to school tomorrow, keep the car, and take these boxes over to Becky's tomorrow night."

Sounded good to me. Denny, Oscar, and some of the other SouledOut men were still leading Bible studies Thursday nights at the juvenile detention center—had been ever since Chris Hickman had been incarcerated for several months two years ago. Now that the kids were out of the house and even Wonka was gone, Thursday nights often felt like solitary confinement—

though I didn't admit it to Denny. To fill up the silence, I usually put on one of Israel and New Breed's CDs and pumped up the volume, or ran upstairs to bother Stu and Estelle.

Well, *this* Thursday I'd stay late at school and grade all my papers *before* I came home, and then I'd go over to the Hickmans', get Becky's boxes out of my hair, and hang out with Florida. Or Becky. Whoever would put up with me. Maybe we could start brainstorming ideas for our Yada Yada reunion party. Like *when*. And *where*. It'd have to be after Christmas, but before school started again . . .

But of course it started to snow early Thursday morning. Morning traffic snarled along like a head full of dreadlocks. "Sorry, babe," Denny said when I let him out at the corner of West Rogers High. "I thought this would be helpful. Got your cell phone in case you need it?"

"Yes, got the cell. Don't worry, I'll be fine." We were now a four-cell-phone family, which seemed ridiculous at times, but I had to admit having my own cell phone had rapidly become indispensable—though I sometimes felt slightly silly standing in an aisle at the grocery store, calling Denny to see if we needed any more onions.

I barely squeaked into the parking lot at Bethune Elementary before the first bell rang, so I felt off-balance most of the day without my usual half hour to quiet my spirit, pray for my students, glance over my lesson plans, or read the daily staff bulletin.

But the last bell finally rang, and I was grateful to kick back in the quiet classroom with a cup of hot instant soup, courtesy of the teachers' lounge microwave. I prayed for two of my students, both of whom had hacking coughs and had probably infected half the

class; finally read the staff bulletin, which informed me I was supposed to turn in midterm grades by next Friday; picked up the
usual assortment of "left behind" items—a hat, three unrelated
mittens, a wet sock, homework pages that were supposed to go
home, and a Game Boy with no batteries; and finally tackled the
stacks of book reports and math homework I had to grade.

It was dark outside by the time I finished grading papers,
packed up my tote bag, and headed for the parking lot. The janitor
had to let me out, but at least I had the car and didn't have to walk
home. I felt good. My tote bag felt light. I hummed a wobbly version of "It Is Well With My Soul," wishing I could remember all
the verses of that grand old hymn.

The snow had stopped, but I still drove at fifteen miles an hour
on the icy side streets, which hadn't been plowed or salted, and
probably wouldn't be since it had only snowed a couple of inches.
I decided to go straight to the Hickmans' and get rid of Becky's
boxes, afraid that if I went home first, I wouldn't want to go out
again, and all of Denny's good intentions for leaving me the car
would have been for nothing.

Rats. I forgot about parking. The Hickmans' rented house was
only about six blocks from us, squeezed between a couple of three-
story apartment buildings. Cars lined the curbs bumper to bumper.
I drove around the block, which took me out onto busy Clark
Street, grinned as I passed Adele's Hair and Nails, brightly lit with
twinkling lights in the window, and was tempted by an empty
parking meter. *Nope.* No way could I carry all those boxes in one
load, and I wasn't about to make two trips in this weather.

I'd just about decided to double-park in front of the Hickman
house, unload the boxes, and forget about hanging out with

Florida tonight, when a car pulled out at the far end of their block and its taillights disappeared around the corner. A parking space! *Thank You, Jesus!*

Well, why not? I *was* thankful.

I backed carefully into the parking space, maybe six inches farther out from the curb than I should be, but who cared? Pulling up the collar of my winter jacket and slinging my purse over my shoulder, I picked up the largest set of boxes from the back of the minivan, locked the car, and started gingerly up the slippery sidewalk toward the Hickmans'. I'd send one of the kids out for the other boxes.

Hearing muffled footsteps running behind me, I walked a bit faster. *Wish I'd parked closer to the house—*

Without warning, my feet flew out from under me as someone jerked my purse off my shoulder with the full force of a run. I didn't have time to think before I spun around and crashed to the icy sidewalk on my back, the boxes flying out of my hands. Pain shot up my leg, as if I'd been stabbed by a hot knife . . . my left leg! The one I'd broken in the accident . . . but the pain shot up from my ankle, which was twisted under my body.

I let out a cry of pain—just as I saw two more figures headed straight for me. Terrified, I threw up my arms to protect my face . . . but the two figures, bundled up against the cold, simply parted as if I was a traffic island and kept running.

They weren't going to hurt me! I tried to get up, but the pain pushed me down. "Help! My ankle! . . . Somebody, help me!" Hot tears squeezed from my eyes. "Ohh," I groaned. "My ankle . . . I can't . . ."

Far down the block I heard someone yell, "Boomer! Whatchu doin'? *Come on!*"

I twisted my head, trying to see. But pain and tears blurred my vision. I tried again to get up, but the pain was too great. No way was I going to walk on this ankle. *Oh God, help me . . . help me . . .*

Again that voice, further away. "Boomer, you *idiot!* Get outta there! . . . We're leavin', man!" The voice faded.

Cold seeped through my slacks. I started to shiver. I had to get out of here . . . my cell phone! I had my cell phone! Frantically I patted my jacket pockets . . . nothing. *Oh no! Did I put it in my purse? . . . No.* I distinctly remember putting it in my pocket, with my keys—

A head crossed my vision. I couldn't see a face—just a hooded jacket and knit cap pulled low, the face in shadow. But someone was bending over me.

I flinched . . . then gasped, "Help me . . . please. I'm hurt. I need my cell phone. I . . . lost it when I fell. Do you see it?"

The figure straightened. Had to be just a teenager. He looked about, and then bent down and picked up something . . . my phone! He flipped it open and punched the keys. I heard three beeps, then a Send tone. *Three beeps?* "What—?"

But before I could ask who he was calling, the person set the phone down on the ground about six inches from my fingers . . . and ran.

7

For half a second, I forgot the pain in my ankle. *What in the world—?*

Then I heard a faraway voice. "9-1-1 operator. What"—I snatched the phone off the ground and put it to my ear—"is your emergency?"

"Uh, uh . . . I'm sorry. Dialed by mistake. Sorry." I fumbled with my cold fingers, managed to flip the phone closed. The lighted LED died. I let my head fall back to the snowy sidewalk. No way did I want to lie here for ten minutes waiting for paramedics to arrive, and it was probably just a sprained ankle anyway. The Hickmans were just up the street. That's what I needed to do—call Florida and Carl, tell them I'm lying out on their sidewalk, feeling like a fool.

Good thing I had the Hickmans' number on speed dial. My brain felt like cold oatmeal. And the pain in my ankle robbed me of lucid thought. Carl was at my side in half a minute, no coat, Florida right behind him. I was so glad to see them, I started to cry.

"Jodi Baxter! What—? Never mind. I'm gonna call 9-1-1."

"No, no," I gasped. "It's just a sprained ankle. Just get me to your house. Please."

Between the two of them and me hobbling on one foot, they got me inside. I sank down on their couch, winced as Florida pulled off my boot, but gratefully accepted the pillows she used to prop up my left foot. "Ice," she muttered. "Gotta get ice on that foot. Carl, where you goin'?"

"Goin' to pick up Jodi's stuff lying out there on the sidewalk. I saw a bunch of boxes. Those yours? What else is out there? You got your purse?"

I shook my head. "I was bringing boxes for Becky. But my purse . . . it's gone. That's what happened. Somebody ran up behind me, grabbed my purse, made me fall down . . ." I blinked back hot tears, suddenly feeling the full weight of fear and pain now that I was inside and safe and among friends.

Both Carl and Florida stared at me. "I'm calling the police," Carl muttered.

"No, wait! I . . . give me a minute to think, please?" I wanted to stay on the Hickmans' couch. I didn't want police standing around in their living room asking questions.

Carl scratched his head. Like Denny. Did all men do that when they felt frustrated? Then he yelled up the stairs. "Chris! Cedric! Get down here! I need some help!"

The two boys came clattering down the stairs—and stopped, staring at me propped up on the couch. "What's wrong, Mrs. B?" At sixteen, Chris Hickman had shot up as tall as his dad—and was as good-looking.

"Don't you be askin' no questions," Florida scolded on her way to the kitchen. "Just git on outside, help your dad pick up Mrs. Baxter's things. She . . . fell."

"Wait!" I sniffled, fumbling in my jacket pockets until I found my car keys. "There's a bunch more empty boxes in the back of my car. Can you bring 'em in, Chris? They're for Becky."

Florida came back with a plastic bag full of ice cubes wrapped in a dishtowel and packed my foot, muttering the whole time. "You're a stubborn woman, Jodi Baxter. You need to get this x-rayed. What if it's broken? An' if you don't report a purse snatchin' to the police, then I'm goin' to. Don't want no thief workin' *my* block. Whatchu got in that purse, anyway—credit cards? You gotta call the credit card companies and put a stop on 'em, else that thief gonna rack up several hundred bucks tonight 'fore you can blink."

"Thieves," I said.

"What?"

"There were three of them. One came back to help me."

Florida stared at me. "What do you mean, came back?"

I tried to explain what happened. "I'm not positive the person who found my phone was one of the thieves, except somebody kept yelling at him to run. But he found my phone and dialed 9-1-1."

"What? That's what I'm talkin' about. You should be on your way to the hospital. Wait—if he called for an ambulance, how come I don't hear no sirens out there?"

"Um . . . I ended the call. Called you instead."

Florida threw up her hands. "Lord, help me here 'fore I slap this girl upside the head. I have half a mind to throw you right back outside on the street."

WELL, I GOT to hang out with the Hickmans that evening, all right. Carl wouldn't hear of taking me home and leaving me alone, even though I was anxious to find our credit card numbers and get the cards cancelled. He finally got through to Denny, who'd had his cell phone shut off while he was inside the juvenile detention center; Oscar Frost dropped him off at the Hickmans' around nine-thirty.

Tight-lipped, my husband agreed with Florida, called the police to report a purse-snatching-with-injury, and told the dispatcher we'd meet them at the emergency room of St. Francis Hospital. "What about the credit cards?" I winced as he and Carl helped me out to our minivan. "Shouldn't we go home first, make some calls?"

"Did it already. I have my cards, remember? And Oscar was driving."

"Oh." Something told me Denny was in no mood to be questioned right now.

We didn't get home until almost midnight. "Told you it was just a sprain," I mumbled as he helped me into the house. "How much is this going to cost us?"

"Jodi Marie Baxter. I don't care! It's a *bad* sprain, you've got a torn ligament, it could've been worse, and now we both know you have to stay off it totally for *at least* two days, and on crutches for a week." He rattled the discharge papers at me. "I've got it all here in black and white. Besides . . ." He picked me up and carried me into the bedroom, and started helping me out of my clothes. "Just say you did it for my sake."

He leaned forward and fixed me with his gray eyes. His voice gentled. "You scared me half to death, Jodi. You didn't just fall down. You were mugged. It's a violent crime! I just thank God that you're . . . " He stopped. And then grinned.

"What?"

"Um, did anyone at the Hickmans' tell you that your mascara is all smudged? You look like a raccoon."

DENNY CALLED BETHUNE Elementary first thing Friday morning to say I was "laid up," and was going to take a sick day himself to stay home with me. "I know you. You'd be up and down all day, trying to get stuff done. Ain't gonna happen, babe. That recliner is your throne until further notice." But Florida must have tattled to Yada Yada while we were at the hospital, because Estelle came downstairs and offered to "Jodi-sit." Her most recent elder care patient had passed away, and she didn't start a new assignment until Monday.

"Leave her to me, Denny," she said, waving him out the door. "I've got experience with ornery patients."

Except for the dull throb in my ankle and aching all over from the fall, it was kind of nice being waited on hand and foot. Estelle seemed to anticipate when I needed another cup of coffee, brought me pain medicines when I needed them, and chatted with me just enough to be companionable, but she didn't hover over me every minute. In fact, she lugged Stu's sewing machine downstairs, set it up on our dining room table, and sewed away on one of her sewing projects while I read.

Dozing in the recliner after lunch—homemade corn chowder and hot biscuits—my mind drifted to what had happened the night before. *Being jerked off my feet . . . falling . . . muffled footsteps running away . . . then the shadowy figure bending over me . . . some-one yelling in the distance, "Boomer, you idiot! Run!"*—

I opened my eyes. *Boomer.* That must be the name of the person who came back! Why didn't I remember that last night when the police officer asked me if I could identify the thieves in any way? Should I call him back? The officer had given me his card in case I remembered anything else.

But something inside me checked. Maybe there had been three thieves. But the person who came back wasn't the one who'd grabbed my purse. My gut was sure of that. And he'd come back. And tried to help. No, I wasn't going to call . . .

But you can pray, Jodi. Pray for Boomer. Like you did for Sara, even before you knew her name . . .

"Estelle? Can you come here a sec?"

The *whirring* in the other room stopped. Estelle appeared in the living room archway. "What you need, baby?"

"Nothing. I just wondered . . . would you help me pray for Boomer?"

ESTELLE MADE SUPPER from stuff she found in our kitchen—smothered pork chops and corn pudding—and Stu joined us when Denny got home; it felt almost like a party. But by Saturday, I was plenty tired of just sitting in the front room recliner with my foot in the air and answering phone calls from well-meaning friends.

"Keep that foot elevated at least another day, Jodi," Delores cautioned. "Keep icing it, too, but only ten minutes at a time, and then rewrap."

Avis called. "Don't worry about school on Monday, Jodi. We've already got a sub lined up for you."

"Never wear de purse over just one shoulder, Sista Jodee," Chanda scolded. "Over your head and inside de coat, next time."

"Who needs a purse?" Yo-Yo snorted. "Just stuff what you need in your pockets. Works for me." Right. Yo-Yo always wore overalls.

"Boxes, schmoxes," Ruth sputtered in my ear. "Half your age, Becky is. Let her get her own boxes. I'm coming over with chicken soup." . . . "I'm not sick, Ruth." . . . "So? You need to be sick to eat chicken soup?"

When the phone rang for the tenth time that day, I hollered at Denny, "If that's Becky again"—she'd already called twice, saying it was all her fault—"tell her I'm on my way to Colorado to go skiing!"

Denny brought me the phone. "It's Josh."

"Oh . . . Hi, honey."

"Sorry about your fall, Mom. And getting your purse snatched. Must have been scary."

"Yes, I—"

"I called to ask you and Dad to pray. And feel free to pass it on to Yada Yada."

So much for being fawned over by one's offspring. "Sure, honey. What's wrong?"

"Carmelita's missing again."

I WOKE IN the middle of the night, my ankle throbbing, and got up to take some pain meds, using the crutches we still had from when I broke my femur. Heating a mug of milk in the microwave, I peeked out the window in the back door. Snowing again. So much for going to church in the morning. Walking on crutches indoors was one thing; crutches on snow and ice was another.

Settling in the recliner with my foot up, swathed in an afghan, I tried to go to sleep again . . . but all I could think about was Carmelita. Was she out somewhere in this snow? Drugged out, messed up, in grave danger of losing her baby? *Oh God! Help them find her, Lord!* Who was taking care of the baby, anyway? Edesa probably. Couldn't be easy for her. She was going to school, had homework and classes and papers to write.

Huh. Sure put my sprained ankle—even having my purse stolen—into perspective.

Oh God! Thank You for Your blessings, even in the midst of this situation! Forgive me for complaining about all the phone calls. I'm truly blessed to have so many friends and family who care about me. Thank You for Estelle, who took care of me Friday. For Ruth's chicken soup. For Florida and Carl . . . even for Boomer, whoever he is, who stopped to find my phone. Bless him for that, Lord. But God, Josh and Edesa and everyone at Manna House are worried about Carmelita . . . I don't know her story, Lord, but You do. You know where she is now. Even if she's in a dark place, You are there . . .

I grabbed my Bible. Psalm 139. Yes, I would pray Psalm 139 for Carmelita.

I STAYED HOME from church, which meant missing the second Advent service at SouledOut, but by Sunday evening I was going stir-crazy. I think I was starting to drive Denny crazy, too, because he gave in and drove me to the Hickmans', where Yada Yada was meeting. The snow had only added another inch or two, and by then even most of the side streets had been plowed.

After getting me into the house and settled on the couch, Denny coaxed Carl to go out with him for pizza; at the last minute, they took Chris, Cedric, and Carla too. I noticed Florida had a new hairstyle since I saw her three days ago—little sections of hair twisted into knots all over her head. "What do you call that?" I ran my finger in tiny circles. "It's cute."

"Zulu knots. Like it?" Florida simpered as she ran to answer the doorbell.

Ruth arrived *sans* twins—but Delores and Edesa arrived *with* a bundle in a baby carrier. My heart lurched. "Oh, Edesa, does that mean Carmelita hasn't come back yet?"

"Not yet. We are very worried." Edesa took off her own winter wraps, then gently unsnapped the safety strap of the carrier and picked up the baby, blankets and all. "Do you want to hold *la bebé*, Jodi?"

"Me? Um . . . sure." I peeked into the warm, fleece blankets Edesa put into my arms. The baby's dark lashes lay against her fat cheeks, damp, dark curls wisping around her face. *"The baby"* . . . *why did I always refer to her that way? She had a name—Gracie.* For some reason, a lump tightened in my throat.

As the Yada Yadas arrived, they oohed and ahhed over the baby in my arms, plying Edesa for details. But Avis interrupted. "I'm sure Edesa doesn't want to have to repeat herself. Let's go ahead and begin, and then we'll hear from Edesa first thing."

After Avis's brief prayer, Edesa brought the group up to date about Carmelita showing up at Manna House the day of the dedication, her disappearance on Thanksgiving and return, her tears and promises to stick with the detox program she'd started last Monday . . . and now, gone again. She'd been missing more than twenty-four hours.

"We went through the things in her room, hoping to find some clue to where she might have gone. But"—Edesa's voice wavered—"all we found was this." She took an envelope out of her pocket and pulled out a single sheet of paper. Her lip trembled.

"Here." Delores gently took the paper from Edesa's hand. "I will read. It is written in Spanish." The older woman frowned as she translated. "'*Por favor*, if anything should happen to me, I give the care of my baby, Gracie Francesca Alfaro, to Edesa Reyes at Manna House.'" Delores looked up. "It is signed, 'Carmelita Francesca Alfaro.'"

8

hoa." Stu's eyes went wide. "Did you know about this, Edesa?"

Edesa shook her head. She reached over and tenderly stroked the baby's cheek with the back of her fingers. "I just hope we find your mama, *niñita*," she whispered.

The sisters gathered around Edesa and the baby I was holding and prayed, pouring out their hearts for the young, lost mother and her abandoned baby. By the end of the prayers, we'd used up half a box of Florida's tissues.

The group also prayed for rapid healing of my sprained ankle, and for Becky and Little Andy as they prepared to move from the cocoon of the Hickman household to their own apartment. "Thanks for the boxes, everybody," Becky said sheepishly. "Though I wish Jodi hadn't—"

"Give it a rest, Becky!"

"Okay, okay. Um, I hate to ask, but I'm movin' a week from Saturday if anyone has a couple of hours to help. Ah, except Jodi."

"Becky Wallace!" I rolled my eyes. "Will someone stuff a sock in her mouth?"

Becky sniffed self-righteously. "Well, you *can't* help, even if you wanted to."

Florida leaned my way. "That's the men's breakfast Saturday," she murmured in my ear. "Think we can volunteer them?"

Before the meeting ended, we talked about Nony's e-mail, bemoaning the short visit but agreeing it'd be best to have our reunion celebration after Christmas. "What about New Year's Day—that's a Sunday," Stu suggested. "That's our regular Yada Yada time, first Sunday of the month. Weekend would be best for everybody anyway."

"Just we sistas? Or invite de 'usbands and de kids?" Chanda stuck out her lip in an exaggerated pout. "Dem *wit'* 'usbands, anyway."

We laughed, but agreed on husbands and kids, lots of food, lots of music, time to share, time to worship and pray . . . exact time and place still to be decided.

"*Humph.* You *know* dat Nonyameko going to be all decked out, wit' dem blue-an'-gold outfits from Sout' Africa and dose head-dresses she wear," Chanda said. "Well, mi too. Going to dress like de Jamaicans dress when we party."

Yo-Yo snickered. "Uh-huh. Only problem, Chanda. Your snowboots gonna look mighty funny with those sleeveless beach dresses you brought back last time."

I STAYED HOME on Monday, since Avis had already arranged for a substitute, but I told Denny I wanted to go to school on Tuesday if he'd give me a ride. "I'll get Avis or somebody to give me a ride home . . . I promise," I added.

When I arrived at school, hobbling into my classroom on crutches, a stack of handmade get-well cards from my students sat on my desk. *How sweet.* Another teacher brought my students from the gym when the bell rang, and the kids seemed excited to see me, examining the soft "boot" with Velcro straps I was wearing on my left foot and wanting to know, "Didja like *my* card?" and, "Can I try your crutches?"

But the novelty of having me back wore off soon enough, and I found myself raising my voice more than I wanted to, simply because it was too much effort to walk around the classroom supervising their desk work as I usually did. Avis, bless her, showed up unannounced and just hung out in my classroom for ten minutes before lunchtime, walking between the clusters of desks, giving smiles and nods—and a few frowns when needed. And after lunch, she sent Ms. Ivy from the school office to do the same thing.

But by the time the last bell rang, my foot was throbbing and I was pooped. Avis said she'd give me a ride home, but it'd be four o'clock before she could leave. Fine with me. I tanked up on ibuprofen, propped my foot on an upturned wastebasket, and used the time to grade papers and plan for the next day . . .

The next day? *Sheesh.* I'd barely made it through this one.

But I enjoyed the five minutes I had Avis all to myself as she drove me home in her toasty warm Camry. "How's Rochelle doing?"

She glanced sideways at me. "You saw her the last time I did, at the dedication for Manna House. I think she's tired of being 'poor

Rochelle' . . . out to prove she's not going to let HIV stop her from living a full life. And she's doing a pretty good job of it too. She loves her job working retail at one of the boutiques in downtown Chicago. All glamour and upscale." She slipped me a wry grin. "Can't afford the clothes myself." The grin faded. "I just wish she'd find a good church and settle down."

"She was coming to SouledOut for a while. Conny seemed to love it."

"Yes, he did. And it was a nice way to see them both every week without being in each other's hair." Avis sighed, but kept her eyes on the street as she turned into Lunt Avenue, which was one-way. "To tell you the truth, Jodi, I think my other daughters feel neglected ever since Rochelle was diagnosed. Peter and I are thinking of driving to Cincinnati to see Charette and Bobby and the twins for Christmas. Tabitha and Toby are in first grade now! They've invited Rochelle and Conny to come, and Natasha too—though she's living in New York since she graduated. We'll see."

"Christmas! When are you coming back? In time for our Yada Yada reunion, I hope."

"Don't worry. Wouldn't miss it for the world." Avis double-parked in front of my house and kept the car running as she got out. "Stay there, Jodi. I'm coming around to get you."

There wasn't much Avis could do except hold my tote bag as I used my crutches to boost me up the porch steps, one at a time. "Thanks. I'll be fine now."

"No problem. I'll wait till you get inside."

I opened the storm door and started to insert my keys in the lock, when I noticed something had been wedged between the two doors. "What's this?"

"I'll get it." Avis bent down and picked it up. We both stared at it. Avis was holding my stolen purse.

WE STILL HAD leftovers from the food various Yada Yada sisters had dropped off that weekend. Denny dished out individual plates when he got home, and while waiting for them to reheat in the microwave, I showed him the purse Avis and I had found on our doorstep.

"How weird is that? Everything's here—my wallet, ID, insurance card, lipstick, address book, coupons . . . except for the cash and credit cards, of course."

"*Huh*. Of course." The microwave beeped and Denny carried the two plates to the dining room table.

"But why bother to return the purse? I mean, I'm glad to have it back, and my other stuff, but don't purse snatchers just take what they want and toss the purse?"

Denny grinned. "I don't know. It's been a long time since I've snatched any purses. I forget the drill."

"Denny! Be serious! . . . Anyway, let's say thanks and eat. I'm hungry." I leaned my crutches against the table, sank into a chair, and closed my eyes. "Lord, thank You for this food and for the friends who brought it, and thanks I didn't have to cook it. And Lord, thanks that thief returned my purse . . ." My eyes flew open. "Wait a minute! Why am I assuming the thief returned it? The thieves probably tossed it in the bushes, but some Good Samaritan found it, saw my wallet and ID with my name and address, and dropped it off. That has to be it!" I closed my eyes again, grinning. "So . . . yes, Lord, bless the Good Samaritan who found my purse and returned it. You know who he or she is. Return their kindness many times over—"

The phone rang, interrupting my extended prayer. "Thank goodness," Denny muttered, jumping up to get the phone. "I thought you were hungry . . . Hello? Baxters . . . Oh, hi, Josh. What's up?" Denny listened a long time. I saw his features sag and he glanced at me. "I'm so sorry, Josh . . . Yeah, sure, sure. It's fine. See you tomorrow night." He slowly put the phone back in its cradle.

"Denny? What? Is it—?"

Denny nodded, sat back down in his chair, and pushed his plate away. "It's Carmelita. They found her . . . dead. Drug overdose. Found her in a drug house about two blocks away from the shelter."

I just stared at my husband. *Carmelita . . . dead? Oh God! How could this happen! Didn't we pray for her safety?* I felt angry . . . and confused. God had answered so many of our prayers! Why not this one? All the people praying for Carmelita certainly satisfied the promise Jesus had made: "If two of you agree on anything . . . my Father in heaven will do it"—several times over!

I put my head in my hands. *Oh God, I don't understand . . .*

A few moments later, I looked up at Denny. "What did you mean when you told Josh, 'See you tomorrow night'?"

"He asked if he could come by tomorrow night for supper. Said he needed to talk."

"Just Josh?"

"That's what he said."

I DID GO to school the next day and managed a little better physically. Still couldn't put any weight on my left foot, but I moved around on my crutches more freely and didn't get as tired. But emotionally . . . I had a hard time focusing on division problems and arid regions of the earth. My mouth said the right things to the students ("Hand in your geography worksheets" . . . "Who wants to work the problem on the board?"), but my mind and heart kept up a running prayer with God.

Lord Jesus, please don't let Josh hit another skid over Carmelita's death . . . He takes things so personally . . . And what's going to happen to Carmelita's baby? . . . Jesus, have mercy on little Gracie. She's so innocent, but she's had such a hard life already . . . Maybe they can find the father . . . but he's probably some no-good jerk who abandoned Carmelita when he found out she was pregnant . . . Oh God, in Your great love and mercy, Gracie needs You now . . .

Avis took me home again. We sat in front of my house in her car as the streetlights came on, holding hands with the heater running, and prayed for Manna House, its staff and volunteers and residents, facing yet another trauma. " . . . And Father, we *thank You* for what You are going to do in baby Gracie's life," Avis prayed. "Thank You for bringing her to a safe place before her mother died. Help those who care for her to bear fruit in every good work. And help Gracie to grow up in the knowledge of You and to be strengthened with Your power. Rescue her, Lord, from the kingdom of darkness that took her mother, and bring her into the kingdom of light . . . "

After an *amen*, Avis glanced at me and grinned. "I've been reading the first chapter of Colossians."

O-kay. I was going to have to reread Colossians, find all that good stuff.

Denny brought home takeout from Eng's Asian Cuisine on

Western Avenue, a large order of General Tso's chicken with rice and one order of Thai spicy chicken wings, which was more than enough for the three of us and cost ten bucks. Josh arrived shortly, his nose and ears red from his walk from the Morse Avenue el station. He looked around as he shed his knit hat and jacket. "Seems kind of lonesome around here without Willie Wonka. You guys thought of getting another dog?"

Every day. "Sometimes. But we're at work all day and you kids are both at school . . . Come on, sit down. Food's hot."

We made small talk while Denny served up the chicken and spicy wings—how long I'd have to be on crutches, how Josh's classes were going, how the West Rogers High Panthers were doing this year without their basketball stars from last year's senior class. But Josh didn't seem to be eating much, just pushing his food around on his plate.

"What's up, Josh?" Denny finally cut through the small talk. "You said you wanted to talk."

Josh sighed and pushed his plate away. "Yeah." He blew out a long breath, as if letting out something bottled up inside. "Edesa wants to adopt Gracie."

His announcement hung suspended in the air for a long, startled moment . . . then words tumbled from my mouth before they were even complete thoughts. *"Adopt?"* But, but . . . that's a huge decision! She shouldn't feel obligated just because of Carmelita's note. Carmelita didn't even *ask* her! Oh, Josh. Manna House needs to call DCFS, if they haven't already. I'm sure Illinois has all sorts of laws and regulations in a case like this. Indigent mother; abandoned baby. Maybe there are other relatives—"

"I *know*, Mom. I feel so confused. Edesa cried and cried when

82

they found Carmelita. But now . . . it's like she's got her mind made up. She feels responsible for Gracie. More than that. A commitment. She's really bonded to the kid, feels that God brought Carmelita and Gracie into her life for a reason. But . . . " The pain on Josh's face was palpable. "Where do *I* fit into this?"

9

*M*y heart ached. "Oh, Josh." Leave it to my big mouth to blab away before I even listened to what he was feeling. *Oh God, please help me curb my knee-jerk tendency.*

Denny's brows knit together. "Go ahead, son."

Josh talked and we listened for the next half hour. "I still have a couple of years before I get my BA, and Edesa's got another year of school at least . . . We haven't even set a *wedding* date, much less talked about starting a family! . . . But she's my fiancée; doesn't this affect me too? . . . What if she adopts the baby now, or even becomes the foster mom? Doesn't that leave me out? . . . But if I say it's a bad idea, and she's determined . . ." Josh's head sank into his hands. "Oh God! I don't want to lose her."

It was several minutes before I trusted myself to speak. Denny's face was furrowed with concern. I realized now that Josh didn't need our opinions. He needed us to *care*. And to pray with him for wisdom. He needed us to pray for Edesa and for Carmelita's baby girl and this whole, sad, complicated situation. To help carry the burden he was carrying right now.

The three of us held hands—Josh gripped ours as if holding on for dear life—and we prayed and cried together. When he finally pushed his chair back and reached for his jacket, Denny said he'd drive him to the el station.

"Just a word of advice, son. Encourage Edesa to talk with others she considers her spiritual mentors."

"Delores," I blurted. "She should talk with Delores Enriquez."

Denny nodded. "Delores would be good. But the *most* impor-tant thing is, whatever the decision, the two of you should make it together."

FOR ONCE, I didn't get on the computer and send an e-mail to the whole Yada Yada list asking for prayer—though it was tempting to unleash the prayer warriors. But I felt God's Spirit holding me in check. *Just pray, Jodi. That's your job right now.*

But what am I supposed to pray? I'm not exactly unbiased. Josh is my son, after all. I have his well-being at heart.

What about Edesa, Jodi? She's part of his heart now. Can you trust Me with your son and your future daughter-in-law?

Could I? I wanted to. But I knew I could use some help. Avis. She already knew about Carmelita's death. Swinging into her office on my crutches the next morning before school started, I shut the door and blurted, "Edesa wants to adopt Gracie."

To her credit, Avis's mouth made an O. Then she said, "Oh my."

Well, at least I didn't have to explain it to her. "Please, just pray for Josh and Edesa right now. Josh is upset and confused. *They* need a lot of wisdom, and *I* need to trust God and keep my big nose out of it."

Avis smiled. "At least you're honest."

"Huh! You didn't have to agree with me—about the big nose, anyway." I wiggled my nose between thumb and forefinger. "Is it really . . .?"

"Jodi! That's not what I meant. Come on, let's pray. The bell's about to ring."

I FELT ENCOURAGED after praying with Avis. Funny how God had used Yada Yada—this curious prayer group of multiflavored sisters—to teach me so much about the importance of the body of Christ and how much the different parts need each other. Avis even agreed that the rest of Yada Yada should *at least* be told about Carmelita's death—and she offered to make the calls herself, to let me off the hook.

But even I was distracted from the drama going on at Manna House by the snowstorm that blew in while I was still at school that day. A heavy fog blanketed the entire metro area, as if the snow clouds were so loaded, they just sank down on the city. When the fog finally lifted the next day, we had eleven inches of new snow.

But did they cancel the public schools? Ha! This was Chicago. I would have loved to walk to school on Friday and savor the quiet beauty of new snow weighing down the broad arms of the occasional fir tree, like a picturesque Christmas card. But Denny had to drive me; I still couldn't put much weight on my sprained ankle. At least the city snowplows had arrived during the night and plowed out the municipal parking lots, including the schools, leaving six-foot snow mountains in various spots, much to the delight of the kids playing King of the Mountain.

Avis drove me home again. Denny didn't get home until late, saying he'd shovel our walks in the morning. I was looking forward to a day at home, back in the recliner with my foot up. But Josh called that night, saying they were having a funeral for Carmelita at Manna House on Saturday morning and could his dad be one of the pallbearers?

I knew it was a sacrifice for Denny to have to put on a suit and tie on a Saturday morning. But he agreed I could stay home. "Right. You shouldn't push it, Jodi. Josh and Edesa will understand. You put in a four-day workweek on crutches. Give yourself a break." He shrugged into his overcoat and pecked me on the cheek. "Sorry about the sidewalks . . . but at least you're not going anywhere."

Stu called, asking if she and Estelle could ride with us. Denny hustled out to the garage, collar up, wading through the drifts, with Stu and Estelle stepping right behind him in his man-size footprints. I sank into the recliner a few minutes later, grateful that Denny understood without me having to convince him. Yes, I needed a day to rest as my ankle was healing . . . but he knew it would be difficult for me to be there, seeing Edesa with the baby, knowing the inner turmoil Josh was going through, having to make nice, pretending this huge decision wasn't hanging over their heads. Even if there was more to talk about, Carmelita's funeral wasn't the place to do it.

Was I being a wimp? Probably. At least I had a quiet morning for some much-needed prayer and Bible reading. *That* part of my day had been buried all week by the weather, early schedules, and the sheer annoyance that everything I did took longer on crutches.

For a while I just sat, soaking up the quiet. Praying for those at the funeral, and yes, praying for Carmelita's baby, that a good home could be found for her. Praying for Josh and Edesa and their future, praying for Amanda, who would be home in another week for her monthlong winter break . . .

Whoa. It was December tenth already. Only two weeks until Christmas! We didn't have our tree. I hadn't done any shopping— *couldn't* do any shopping until I was more mobile. We hadn't done any decorating except for getting out our Advent wreath table centerpiece. When was I going to—

Jodi, Jodi, Jodi. The Voice in my spirit cut into my rising tide of anxiety. *Is that what Christmas is all about?*

Well, no, but—

It's My birthday! You love to celebrate birthdays. How are you going to celebrate My birthday this year? I don't need much. I had a pretty simple birth, you know—stable, feed trough, common folks. Of course, there were those magi who showed up with some awesome gifts . . .

I smiled, my muscles relaxing. Okay, good reminder. Christmas is Jesus' birthday. And yes, I loved to celebrate birthdays for my family and Yada Yada sisters. I'd been having fun the last few years digging up the meaning of everyone's names and creating a card or gift to go with the names . . .

My smile grew bigger. God had many names, didn't He? I'd never really explored the names of God and what they meant. As long as I was anchored to this chair, why not look up some of the meanings of His names, for His birthday?

89

Excited, I found my fat study Bible and started to dig. *Elohim, "God the Creator"... El Roi, "The God Who Sees Me"* (Whoa. I'd never heard that one before) ... *Jehovah Jireh, "The Lord Will Provide"... Immanuel, "God with Us"... Abba, "Father. Daddy. Papa"*—

The front doorbell derailed my thoughts. *Huh.* I wasn't expecting anyone. Probably the Jehovah's Witnesses or some political petition. I returned to jotting my notes. If I ignored it, they'd go away.

The doorbell rang again. I sighed. Maybe it was the mail carrier needing a signature or something. I dumped my Bible and notebook on the small table beside the recliner, grabbed my crutches, and made for the door. I peeked through the peephole. Oh. Just a kid with a shovel, probably trying to earn some money. I snickered. Good thing Denny wasn't here; he always said no, as if it was an affront to his manhood. Me? I was a sucker for kids trying to earn money.

I opened the door. "Yes?"

"Morning. Would you like your walk—" The kid suddenly grinned big. "Miz B? *You* live here?"

Did I know this kid? I opened the frosty storm door so I could get a better look at him. He was wearing the typical winter gear of urban boys: knit hat, hooded sweatshirt under a padded team jacket. The boy pushed the hood of his sweatshirt back, still grinning. "Don't you recognize me, Miz B?" And there he stood, big as life. A couple of years older, but—

"Hakim Porter!" I threw the storm door open wide. "I can't believe it! Come in! Come in! I was just thinking about you a couple of days ago, wondering what you were up to. And here you are!"

"Oh, uh, don't know if I should come in. I was just lookin' for some shoveling jobs in this neighborhood, and saw your walk needed . . . " His eyes traveled to my crutches, and he suddenly seemed flustered. "What happened, Miz B? You okay?"

"Hakim Porter. Get yourself in here! I'm freezing. *Then* we'll talk."

Reluctantly, he rested his shovel against the porch railing and stepped into the foyer. I shut the door. "Yes, yes, I'm okay. Just fell on the ice, you know. Sprained my ankle." I started into the living room, but realized he wasn't following me. I turned back, leaning on the crutches. "How'd you happen to come to this neighborhood? Do you and your mom live around here?"

Not once since the day I'd said a tearful good-bye to Hakim, when his mother pulled him out of my third-grade classroom to get special tutoring for the learning difficulties he'd been experiencing, had I seen Hakim *or* his mother around this neighborhood or in the stores. I thought they'd moved.

Couldn't blame them. After the accident at the intersection of Howard and Clark Streets, it would be tough to go through that intersection again and again without remembering the tragedy that had taken the life of Hakim's older brother, Jamal.

It was tough for me.

"Uh, not really," Hakim was saying. "Sometimes I stay with my cousins. But after the snow, I was just walking around, looking for people who needed their walks shoveled." He grinned again. "Like you."

I laughed. "Well, that's the truth. My husband was going to do it, but—hey. Let's surprise him. He'll think I did it." I patted the crutches and laughed again. "How much do you charge? Front *and* back."

He shrugged. "Uh, whatever you want to pay me." He opened the front door. "I'll get started."

MY HUSBAND WAS not fooled. "Okay, how much are we out for *that*?" Denny jerked a gloved thumb toward the backyard and its shoveled sidewalks when he came in several hours later. "I said I'd get it done, Jodi. You didn't have to call someone—"

"Denny!" I held up my hand to silence him. "I didn't call anyone. Hakim Porter showed up on our doorstep, wanting to make some money. I hired him. So shoot me." I gave him a playful shove. "And you can't tell *me* you'd rather be out there shoveling snow, than putting on your slippers, kicking back with a cup of coffee, and watching some basketball on TV."

The dimples appeared on Denny's face. "*Sold* to the highest bidder." He shed his coat, gloves, and boots while I followed him around on my crutches. "Hakim Porter, eh? How did he know where we lived? What's it been, now, since he was in your class—three, four years? How much did you pay him?" He glanced at me as he substituted his slippers for the boots. "He did a good job."

"Whoa. One question at a time. I don't think he knew where we lived—he seemed surprised when I came to the door. And I didn't ask, but I assume he's about eleven years old, probably sixth grade. I gave him twenty dollars."

"*Twenty dollars!*" He sighed. "Never mind. It was a big job."

I followed Denny back into the kitchen, where he popped a bagel into the toaster oven and poured himself a cup of coffee. "So . . . tell me about the funeral."

Denny pursed his lips for a few moments. "Simple. Sad. I think the Manna House Foundation kicked in for the casket and funeral expenses. The police are holding Carmelita's body at the morgue for a few weeks to see if any relatives can be located. If not, she'll probably be cremated."

He read the questions in my mind. "Yeah, I saw Josh. Didn't get to talk to him much, though. He was one of the pallbearers, also Peter Douglass and a couple of guys I didn't know. Edesa was there with Gracie, of course. To tell you the truth, Jodi, I'm surprised DCFS hasn't stepped in and just taken the baby. They have to know about her, since it was the police who found Carmelita . . . say, mail come yet? Haven't seen my paycheck and it should have been here by now. Probably a slowdown because of the weather."

He disappeared in the direction of the front door. *Guess we're done talking.* I didn't really expect he'd get a chance to talk with our son, not at a funeral with other people around. But it'd been three days since Josh came home to talk. I'd love to know if he and Edesa had—

Denny reappeared in the kitchen doorway, the mail in one hand and a twenty-dollar bill in the other. "Found this in the mailbox. Any reason why Hakim didn't want to take your money?"

10

The snow was still deep, but I wasn't about to miss worship two Sundays in a row, crutches or no crutches, especially at Christmastime. Denny let me off right in front of the door of SouledOut Community Church, and I braced myself for the barrage of questions and concern the moment the greeters opened the double-glass doors for me. But "I'll be fine, just slipped on the ice," seemed to suffice, and no one seemed to notice that we brought just a bag of bakery rolls for the Second Sunday Potluck instead of the usual hearty main dish.

"Oh, Sister Jodi!" Rose Cobbs, wife of Pastor Joe Cobbs, bent down and gave me a warm hug after I'd found a seat. Her warm brown skin smelled of gardenias. "Someone told me the Sisulu-Smiths might be coming home soon. I know they were close to you and the Douglasses. Do you have any news?"

I liked "First Lady Rose," though we hadn't become close friends or anything. She was a motherly sort, fifty-something, with grown kids and grandkids, and she "mothered" the merged congregation with a smiling grace I usually found inspiring . . . that is, except for the times I felt annoyed at her seemingly unflappable perfection. Didn't she ever get mad? Pick her nose? Burn the roast?

The Voice in my spirit gave me a slap upside the head. *When was the last time you prayed for Rose Cobbs, Jodi? It's hard to be a pastor's wife! Especially when the congregation is a melting pot of races and cultures. She gets discouraged, just like you do. She needs encouragement, just like you do. Encourage her!*

I hugged her back. "Last I heard, they're coming back to sell their house and return to South Africa on a more permanent basis." I saw her smile fade. "I know. I'm disappointed too. God has used Nony in my life in a big way. I miss her."

Rose Cobbs nodded. "Yes. Nonyameko and Mark used to come to our home to pray for us—before Mark suffered that terrible beating, I mean. They were such an encouragement to Pastor and me . . . " She put on her smile again. "But I just thank God we will get to see them for a little while. When did you say they were coming?"

"They were such an encouragement to Pastor and me" echoed in my head. "Uh, last I heard, they're coming home sometime the week after Christmas." I gave a little laugh. "See? I said 'coming home' too. Nony, no doubt, would say South Africa is home."

"Yes. Yes . . . well, thank you, Sister Jodi."

The Voice in my spirit nudged again. *Encourage her!* I grabbed her hand as Rose Cobbs started to leave. "Sister Rose, could we . . . could we go out for coffee or something sometime? After the holidays maybe. I'd love to hear about those grandkids."

To my surprise, her eyes filled with tears. She took hold of my hand with both of hers. "Yes! I'd like that very much. As for the grandkids . . . " Her voice dropped to a whisper. "Please pray for our oldest. Janiqua, she's autistic—and thirteen now. It's getting very hard for her parents."

Autistic . . . *Oh Lord, I had no idea.*

I pulled out the small notebook I kept with my Bible and wrote *J-a-n-i-k-w-a (sp?)* just as the lights dimmed. Denny joined me in the seat I'd saved for him. The eight teenage girls Amanda had trained took their place at the back with lighted candles. The saxophone opened up with a few bars of "O Come, O Come, Emmanuel," but kept low beneath the words of the young soloist off to the side:

> *O come, thou Key of David, come*
> *And open wide our heavenly home . . .*

Once again, the dancers in their dark skirts and white blouses stepped confidently and in unison up the two aisles between the three sections of chairs.

> *Make safe the way that leads on high*
> *And close the path to misery!*

As the girls fanned out at the front, the hand holding the candle lifted up high, while the other hand pushed backward as if closing a door on misery.

The congregation joined in:

> *Rejoice! Rejoice! Emmanuel*
> *Shall come to thee, O Israel!*

Three pairs of girls stepped forward, each pair lighting one of the candles of the Advent wreath.

Third Sunday of Advent . . . one to go. And then Christmas.

Pastor Clark—a widower who'd been pastor of Uptown Community (mostly white) before we merged with New Morning (mostly black) and became SouledOut Community Church—preached on the Old Testament prophecies that the coming Messiah would be the "Son of David," born in "David's city," Bethlehem. Then he used New Testament scriptures to show how Jesus had fulfilled those prophecies, but He had come as a Servant King, confounding those who'd been expecting a political deliverer and warrior.

"How little we understand the true nature of the kingdom of God," Pastor Clark said as he closed his Bible. "Even today, we still have a hard time comprehending Jesus' teachings that the *last* shall be first, the *least* will be the greatest, the *meek* will inherit the earth, and *dying to self* leads to life."

The praise team closed the service with a slow, worshipful version of "O Little Town of Bethlehem." After Pastor Clark's sermon, the words of the third verse took on more meaning:

No ear may hear His coming,
But in this world of sin,
Where meek souls will receive Him,
Still the dear Christ enters in.

Whew. The promised Messiah definitely showed up in a way the "religious" folks didn't expect—in a stable with the animals. But it was the meek folks—the shepherds—who ran to welcome Him . . .

Afterward, as chairs were pushed back and tables set up for the potluck, I was grateful my sprained ankle gave me an excuse to stay anchored for a few more minutes, thinking about Pastor Clark's sermon. His low-key style didn't compare to Pastor Cobbs's dynamic preaching, and his voice was a bit raspy with age—but the man was deep. And what he said was true: I still struggled to understand God's "upside-down kingdom."

Father . . . Abba . . . Daddy God, I prayed silently as lively commotion swirled around me, *forgive me for being such a knucklehead. Even though I've heard the Christmas story a zillion times, help me to hear the story this year with open ears. I want to know You and Your Son and Your Holy Spirit even more this year. Help me to look for You in unexpected places. And thanks for giving me Yada Yada sisters who aren't afraid to get in my face and—*

"Yo, Jodi!"

I opened my eyes. Florida was snapping her fingers in my face.

"What? I was praying."

"Oh. Sorry." Florida plopped down in a chair beside me. "Thought you'd zoned out. Want me to get you a plate of food? Ruth brought some blintzes, whatever they are. Says it's a family recipe."

I declined with a shake of my head, noticing her "Zulu knots" were still holding. She craned her neck, looking around the room. "Where's Josh at? Haven't seen him for a couple of Sundays. He and Edesa goin' to her Spanish church these days? Thought they was doin' every other Sunday. Sure too bad about that Carmelita girl—an' her leavin' that poor baby without a mama. *Mm-mm.* Wonder what's goin' to happen to her?" Florida prattled on, but now I did zone out.

Exactly what I'd like to know.

AFTER THE POTLUCK, the teens invited any adults to stay who'd like to help them decorate the sanctuary, but Denny and I cut out. "I feel like a wimp, just sitting around not doing anything," I said as Denny took my crutches and hoisted me into the front seat of the minivan.

"That's it! You're a wimp!" Denny grinned at me as he climbed into the driver's side. "I always knew there was something special about you, just couldn't put my finger on it."

He had me laughing by the time we got to the house, listing all my special qualities that had surfaced with my spill on the ice: a Cinderella foot that fit perfectly inside that foam-and-Velcro "slipper"; a sexy swing of the hips as I perfected walking on crutches; a laid-back attitude toward life, letting the laundry pile up; the—

Denny stopped midsentence as we came in the back door. The lights were on and music was playing in the living room. Denny and I looked at each other. "Hello?" he called out.

The music flipped off. "Oh, hey, Mom and Dad." Josh met us in the hallway, shirt hanging out beneath a pullover sweater. "It's just us—Edesa and me. We were waiting for you." He waved us toward the living room.

We stopped in the archway. Just Josh and Edesa *and* baby Gracie.

The baby, swathed in blankets, was asleep on Edesa's lap on the couch. Edesa smiled at us—but her smile trembled. *Dear God, she's scared.* I moved to her side, bent down, and gave her a hug.

She hugged me back. *"Gracias,"* she whispered. The bundle in her arms squirmed, whimpered, and then quieted again.

We all sat. "Uh, might as well get to the point." Josh sat on the edge of the recliner in its "down" position, rubbing his hands together. He kept his eyes on Edesa and the baby. "Edesa and I have decided to get married and adopt Gracie. Together. I mean, adopt her together, so she will have both a mother and a father from the get-go."

I swallowed. "Get married . . . when?"

Josh licked his lips. "As soon as we can pull it together." Now he did look at us. "Uh, Mom and Dad, before you guys say anything, just hear me out. Edesa did not ask me to marry her now so we could do this thing. This is my idea. Uh, actually, it was God's idea."

He must have caught the glance that passed between Denny and me, because Josh threw up his hands. "Hey, I know that sounds crazy. But just listen, okay?"

"We're listening, son," Denny said.

Josh drew in a deep breath. "All right. Christmas is coming up, right? So after the funeral yesterday, I was helping some of the Katrina kids put together a Christmas play to surprise their moms. I was reading the Christmas story to them from the Bible, how Mary was engaged to Joseph, but before they got married, an angel told Mary she would get pregnant and have a baby, God's Son, the promised Messiah. And one of the boys snickered and said, 'Man, bet Joseph got rid of that chick in a hurry.' And I said, 'Yeah, well, he was tempted to because he didn't understand that it was *God* doing this thing.'"

I had an inkling where this was going.

"So I kept reading—say, you got a Bible around here?" Josh pounced on the study Bible I'd left beside the recliner. Turning pages until he found what he wanted, he cleared his throat and read: "'Joseph, her fiancé, being a just man, decided to break the engagement quietly, so as not to disgrace her publicly. As he considered this, he fell asleep, and an angel of the Lord appeared to him in a dream. 'Joseph, son of David,' the angel said, 'do not be afraid to go ahead with your marriage to Mary. For the child within her has been conceived by the Holy Spirit . . .'"

Josh closed the Bible. His eyes were brimming. "Mom . . . Dad. I tell you, as I read that, it was like God shouted in my ear, *Josh! Don't be afraid to marry Edesa, for the child I've given to her is from Me.*'"

The whole room seemed to hold its breath.

But a moment later, Josh got up from the recliner and moved over beside Edesa on the couch, pulling her close. Edesa's dark head leaned against his chest, crying softly. I fished for a tissue. Beside me, Denny blew his nose.

Josh broke the silence. His voice was husky. "Mom and Dad, I know it doesn't make sense, and I'm sure you've got a lot of questions. Believe me, *we* have a lot of questions! What about finishing school? Where will we live? How can we support a family? And I'll be first to admit, those are scary questions. But . . ." Josh's voice rose a notch; the huskiness disappeared, and his chin lifted. "I feel—no, I *know*—God spoke to me. So I'm not afraid."

Beside me, Denny suddenly bent over and began to untie his shoes. I nudged him, a *what-are-you-doing?* nudge.

My husband took off one shoe, then the other, and looked up. "I'm removing my shoes," Denny said, "because we're standing on holy ground."

11

I was startled by Denny's dramatic action. But I felt it too. For several minutes none of us spoke, as if reluctant to disrupt a holy hush. Something was happening right here in our living room I didn't completely understand . . . something spiritual. Beyond my comprehension. The kind of God-event that used to terrify the disciples, like when Jesus came walking on the water in the middle of a storm. But Jesus said, *"Take courage! It is I. Don't be afraid."*

Josh had said it himself: scary questions—but he wasn't afraid. He had spoken with absolute certainty, not knowing whether we would understand. He didn't say it in so many words, but his demeanor was loud and clear: *"This is our decision, whether you agree or not."*

My heart hurt within my chest, swollen with mixed emotions. I was so doggone proud of Josh, stepping forward as a man to take responsibility for this woman and this orphaned child. At the same time, I wanted to shake him. *Josh! Wake up! You aren't Joseph and this baby isn't the Christ Child! Don't be melodramatic!*

Questions . . . oh yes, I had *lots* of questions. But one in particular rose to the surface. Finally, I cleared my throat. "What if Carmelita's family is found, and they want the baby? Even if not, isn't adoption an uphill process? You have to meet certain state standards, have home visits, all that kind of thing. I mean, what if you get married, *bam*, off the bat—and then the adoption falls through?"

Josh and Edesa looked at each other, the look of lovers speaking volumes no one else can hear. Then Edesa spoke. "In my heart, Jodi, I truly believe it was God who brought Carmelita to Manna House. And she chose *me* to care for Gracie if anything happened to her! When Carmelita died, I knew what I had to do. Oh yes, I trembled, not knowing if Josh, or anyone, would understand. But like Mary, I had to say, 'If this is Your will, Lord, so be it.' And then, praise Jesus . . . God spoke to Josh too!"

A smile returned to Edesa's face, sunshine on mahogany, as she held up her left hand with the simple engagement ring Josh had given her. "And whatever happens, Jodi, we had already planned to be married, *si*? We are only moving up the timetable. For all the rest, we need to trust God."

Trust God . . . How could I argue with that?

Not knowing what else to do, I asked if they'd like to stay for supper, even though it was only four o'clock and I was still stuffed from the potluck at SouledOut. They declined. "I've got homework to do." Josh sighed. "Still have classes this week."

"Me too." Edesa shifted the baby. "Takes longer with this *bambino* around."

"Well, *that's* a bit of reality," Denny said dryly—and for some reason it struck us funny, and we all laughed a little too loud and maybe too long.

Denny offered to drive them home—Josh to his apartment near the UIC campus, and Edesa back to Manna House with Gracie—strapping the well-used baby carrier Delores had donated into the car's seat belts. As I watched our minivan back out of the garage and bump out of sight over the icy ruts in the alley, hot tears finally hit the surface. I gave in and blubbered out loud to God.

"God! This feels so crazy! So . . . so backwards! What are they gonna do—get married at a justice of the peace just so they can show a marriage certificate to DCFS? What about a *wedding*? In a church! With . . . with invitations and bridesmaids and a reception and time for the grandparents to attend? All the stuff they could do if they weren't trying to hurry ahead of themselves. Is this *really* Your idea—or did Josh and Edesa just find a convenient scripture to rubber-stamp what they want to do?"

I thumped into the bathroom on my crutches and started the bathwater. A good, hot soak. That's what I needed to calm me down. But as I sank beneath the bubbles a few minutes later, my thoughts were still spinning. *Sure, Josh says he's not afraid—but just wait until he has to pay for groceries and rent and the electric bill with just a high school diploma. Groceries aren't optional!*

I was still in the tub when I heard footsteps in the kitchen. Denny was back. I didn't really want to talk to him right now, so I added more hot water and bubble bath. But as the bubbles fizzled and the bathwater cooled to lukewarm, another reality set in.

Josh was twenty-one. He was an adult. He could make this

huge, life-changing decision, and there wasn't a thing we could do about it.

EVEN THOUGH JOSH and Edesa had told us they were going to get married as soon as they could "get it together," I wasn't prepared for Josh's phone call the next evening.

"Mom? Can you get Dad on the extension? . . . Oh, hi Dad. Just wanted to let you guys know we decided to get married on Christmas Eve afternoon. Reverend Handley said we could use the multipurpose room for the wedding, no problem."

I sank into a dining room chair. *Christmas Eve?* That was less than two weeks away! And Manna House? "Why Manna House?" I blurted.

"Couple of reasons. Most important, we'd like the Manna House residents to come to the wedding. They've been part of the whole scenario since Carmelita and Gracie first arrived here; they feel a certain kinship to the baby. Easiest way for them to attend would be to have the wedding there. But also, a lot of churches have Christmas Eve programs going on that day. Even if the time didn't conflict, there would be rehearsals and stuff going on. This way we won't be in anybody's way."

I stifled a hysterical giggle. A wedding at a women's homeless shelter? At least it wasn't a justice of the peace.

"I know it's short notice, but we'd like to invite the grandparents. Could you give me their phone numbers?"

"Uh, sure. Just a minute." I kept the phone to my ear as I hunted for our address book, glad for something to do. The giggle threatened to surface. I'd love to see Denny's upscale-New-York parents' faces when they got the invitation to their grandson's wedding: *"You are cordially invited to celebrate with us at the Manna House women's shelter."* Except it wouldn't be a formal invitation, just a phone call. Still.

" . . . Edesa's family won't be able to come from Honduras, obviously," Josh was saying. "But Delores is going to be 'mother of the bride.' And Edesa would like Amanda to be her maid of honor. Haven't asked her yet, though. Wanted to let you guys know first."

I fumbled through the address book but had trouble finding the numbers. Everything was happening too fast! Too much! Too quickly! Thoughts bounced around in my psyche, bumping against my stew of emotions. Yes, Josh *was* trying to keep us in the loop. But, a wedding on Christmas Eve? Yesterday, the thought of catching up on gift buying seemed like a big deal. And . . . Amanda the maid of honor? *Ack!* Wearing what? How? . . . Wait. If Edesa was going to have a bridesmaid—

"Who's going to stand up with you, Josh?" *Oh. Did I say that last thought aloud?*

"Well, I've been thinking about that. Since Edesa's asking my sister to stand up with her, I thought I might ask José Enriquez. He's the closest thing to a brother Edesa has here in the States— maybe the closest thing to a brother I'll ever have too."

Hm. Amanda *and* José. Sounded like a plot to me.

"You got those numbers, Mom? Actually, I've got a lot of calls still to make."

"Oh. Sure . . . Speaking of calls, should I tell Yada Yada? Are they invited?"

Josh laughed. "Cool it, Mom. Edesa wants to do that. She's Yada Yada, too, you know."

EXACTLY. EDESA REYES was my Yada Yada sister, had been for three and a half years. I loved her so much. When I first met her, she seemed an exotic creature, not African-American, but African-*South*-American. Fluent in English, but Spanish was her mother tongue. She had come to the States from Honduras to attend college—the first in her family—and she had a heart to help the poor and the homeless in practical ways: healthy living, good nutrition, mothering skills, whatever. And she was a delight! Her effervescent spirit brightened every gathering, like a child blowing bubbles.

And yet, when I realized my son had fallen in love with Edesa, a woman three years older than he, everything got complicated. He'd given her an engagement ring when he was nineteen and she was twenty-two. Now he was twenty-one and she was twenty-four—not exactly teenagers. So why did it feel like they were rushing it? Was I holding Edesa at arm's length, not yet accepting my son's choices?

Oh God, I groaned inwardly as I stowed my crutches in the backseat of Avis's car after school later that week and climbed into the front. *I feel like I got on the wrong train, and I want to get off! Why can't I hear You, Lord? Are You in control here?*

"Are you okay, Jodi?" Avis asked as she pulled out of the school parking lot. "I haven't had a chance to talk to you since Edesa called to say she and Josh are getting married next week." She arched an eyebrow at me. "That's kind of huge."

I snorted. "Yeah. Kind of." I blew out a long breath. "To tell you the truth, Avis, I don't know *how* I feel. Mostly overwhelmed. It's all happening so fast! I feel like a spectator at a NASCAR race. *Zoom, zoom, zoom.*"

"Don't blame you." Avis was silent for the next few blocks. But as she pulled up in front of our house, she put the gearshift in Park and took my hand. "Just remember, my sister, God *will* work His purpose out for our children, even if things don't go the way we'd like them to or follow our timetable. Josh and Edesa are two wonderful human beings who love God and want to serve Him. If you can't trust the decisions they're making, trust the One who is at work in their lives. And praise Him, Jodi. Praise God that He is working *all* things together for the good of those who love Him, even when we can't see it."

I leaned over and gave her a hug. "Thanks, Avis. I needed that." I opened the car door and started to get out, when I suddenly remembered something. "Oh no!" I looked back at her in dismay. "You said you might go to Ohio for Christmas! Is that for sure? Nony and Mark aren't coming until *after* Christmas, and neither is Hoshi, which means they'll miss Josh and Edesa's wedding! But not you too! *Argh!*" I wanted to cry.

Avis grimaced. "*Hm.* I hadn't put that together yet. We were thinking of driving down on Christmas Eve, depending on the weather. What time is the wedding? I don't think Edesa said. If it's the morning or early afternoon . . . " Her brow furrowed for a few moments, then she reached over and patted my arm. "Don't worry."

Don't worry . . . Don't worry . . . Seemed as if my Old Jodi responses of worry-first-pray-later had come out of mothballs. Where was my joy? Where was my faith? I made my way up our shoveled walk on my crutches, but tested my weight on the injured foot as I went up the front steps. Not too bad. Getting better. *Thank You, Jesus. Jesus, I know I haven't been thanking You enough . . .*

I paused at the mailbox and dug out a fat handful of bills, cata-logs, and Christmas cards from organized people. *Christmas cards.* One more thing on my should-have-done-but-haven't list—

Something fell out of the pack of mail in my hand and fell to the porch. *Oh, great. I've got to bend over . . . wait a minute. What's this?* I picked up the two small plastic cards. What in the world?

My stolen credit cards. Returned.

12

I showed the cards to Denny later that evening as I heated up leftover corn chowder for supper. He frowned. "Weird. This doesn't make sense."

"I know. At first I thought, 'Hey, another Good Samaritan found my cards and returned them! There must be more honest people in this world than I thought.'" I tested the soup. Hot enough. "Then I realized that's impossible. There's no address on the cards!—not like my driver's license in the purse."

Denny carried the soup pot to the table. "Unless the same person who returned your purse also returned the cards."

"Yeah. Thought of that too. Which means the person who found my purse kept the credit cards and then had a change of heart. Or what about this?" I paused for effect. "The person who returned my purse is also the purse snatcher."

"Huh. I *suppose* the thief could have had a change of heart."

I snorted. "Not much of one. My money and credit cards were gone, remember? Until now, anyway. Big deal. We canceled the cards that night."

Denny frowned again. "So why return them? Doesn't make sense."

I giggled. "Which is where we started." I grabbed his hand. "Come on, let's pray and eat. I'm starving."

But the returned cards worried me. If it *was* the purse snatcher, then the thief had remembered my address and had been to my home—twice.

THE WEATHER GUY predicted snow for Friday, the day Amanda was supposed to drive home from U of I with a carload of other students. We already had two new inches of the fresh stuff when Avis dropped me off after school—just enough to slow traffic to a crawl . . . with more to come. I called out, "Amanda?" as I let myself in, but the only sign of life was a flashing light on our answering machine. I pushed Play.

"Hi, Mom! Hi, Dad. We're on our way, but it's like a parking lot on the freeway. We're . . . hey, where are we?" I heard her talking to someone else in the car, then she was back. *"Close to Kankakee, I guess. Don't worry. Ought to make it home in time for the wedding next weekend, though . . . just kidding! See you tonight. Bye."*

I pushed Replay, just to hear her voice again.

For some reason I felt weepy. Was I that worried? No . . . well, maybe a little. But if I was honest, coming home to an empty house every night was the pits. Which was ridiculous. Good grief, Denny would be home soon.

So why did I feel so lonely?

I missed Willie Wonka.

Not until our old brown Lab died had I realized how much I

talked to him when the rest of the family wasn't around. He'd always been there to greet me when I came home from school, wriggling his whole body with joy. He followed me around the house, listened to me unwind, wagged his tail when I talked about supper options. *("Whaddya think, Wonka—chicken fettuccine or waffles?")* Sure, I enjoyed time by myself to think, to read, to pray—but time by myself *with* Willie Wonka lying on my feet was a comfort I couldn't quite put into words.

Maybe it was time to get another dog . . .

I shook off the thought. *Get over it, Jodi! You and Denny have been over this before. You both work, a dog would be home alone all day . . .*

I sighed. Time to get off my duff and make a welcome-home supper for Amanda. Chicken and dumplings—one of her favorites.

But as I hobbled around the kitchen in my walking boot, defrosting chicken parts in the microwave and hunting up carrots and celery and onions, I couldn't stop blubbering. *Jesus,* I sniffled, *it's Christmas and nothing feels right. I miss Willie Wonka and I miss Nony and Hoshi . . . and, and I'm so frustrated that we don't have time to plan a decent wedding for Josh, with invitations and a shower . . .*

I tackled the bag of carrots with a peeler, sending the peels flying, and then butchered two large onions until it was hard to tell whether the tears running down my face were the onions or me. *And it's really hard not to be mad at Josh and Edesa for all this topsy-turvy, hurry-scurry. Well, okay, not exactly mad, but I'm really annoyed. Why can't they wait till January, or spring break, or next summer?*

I stopped to blow my nose, washed my hands, and resumed browning the chicken. *And I was really hoping Nony and Mark would come back to stay, and we're hardly going to have time to see them at all, and they're going to miss Josh and Edesa's wedding . . .*

I chucked the vegetables into the pot with the chicken and broth, and banged the lid on top. *Now what?* Oh, the dumplings. I grabbed the bin of flour on the counter, but in my haste, it tipped over and spilled flour all over the counter and onto the floor.

"Argh!" I grabbed the broom and tried to sweep up the flour. "And it's only *one* week till Christmas and I don't have *anything* decorated or bought or wrapped!" The mess on the floor was spreading. "And those stupid kids who snatched my purse and made me sprain my ankle *ruined my whole month*!"

A cold breeze made me whirl around. Denny hesitated in the open back door, briefcase in hand. "Um . . . maybe I should drive around the block again."

At that exact moment, the front door banged at the other end of the house. "I'm ho-ome! Mom? Dad? Hey—where's the Christmas tree? Aren't we going to have a tree this year?"

Amanda! I frantically shooed Denny toward the front of the house, giving me another minute to sweep up the mess.

"I was waiting for you to get home, 'Manda!" Denny's voice trailed his footsteps. "Your mom's still grounded. How about the two of us picking up a tree right after supper?"

BY TEN O'CLOCK that night, we had a "Charlie Brown" Christmas tree standing in our front bay windows, complete with colored minilights and the ornaments collected over the years. A little on the short side and a lot on the scraggly, but hey, it was a tree.

I felt better after dumping my frustrations on God's lap—after all, King David did it all the time in the book of Psalms. But while Denny and Amanda were out scouting for a tree, I'd also taken a cue from David the psalm writer—and Nonyameko, who'd taught me to pray the Scriptures—and reaffirmed what I knew about God.

Propping my Bible open to Psalm 62 while I made hot chocolate for the tree gatherers, I'd prayed along with David: "My soul finds rest in You alone, God. My hope comes from You! You alone are my rock and my salvation. You are my fortress!—I will never be shaken. . . . I will trust in You at all times. I can pour out my heart to You, for God is my refuge."

I'd winced at that. I'd poured out my heart, all right . . . more like ran at the mouth. But I practically sang verses eleven and twelve: "One thing God has spoken, two things have I heard: that You, O God, are strong, and that You, O Lord, are loving."

Wow. Oh, wow. *Strong. And loving.* Yes, God was bigger than all the circumstances that had knocked me off-balance. He'd work it all out. And I knew that however things worked out, it was because of His love . . .

"Mom?" Amanda's voice brought me back to the glittering tree. "You gonna give Josh his ornaments for a wedding present? This will be his and Edesa's first Christmas."

"Ha! He'll have to come take them off the tree himself. Besides, they don't even have a place to live yet, much less set up a Christmas tree—oh, yikes, Denny. Speaking of people in transition . . . Becky Wallace is moving tomorrow! Will you and some of the other guys be able to help her after the men's breakfast?"

Denny kicked back in the recliner with his hot chocolate. "Yep. Carl Hickman got a crew together. She doesn't have that much stuff. And I just recruited Ms. Amanda here from the big metropolis of Champaign-Urbana, where the women are strong and the men are good-look—"

"Da-ad!" Amanda whacked her father with a limp Christmas stocking. "That's Minnesota."

Denny grinned at me over her head. It was good to have Amanda home.

WE PULLED UP in front of the Hickman-Wallace home by ten o'clock the next morning. I came along, figuring I could clean out Becky's refrigerator or take care of Little Andy. A crew of guys from the men's breakfast at SouledOut Community Church was already standing on the porch, bundled up in knit hats and leather gloves, their breath frosty in the sharp chill. One lean figure saw us getting out of the minivan, ran over, grabbed Amanda from behind, and swung her around.

"Josh!" she screeched. She wiggled out of his grasp and gave her brother a bear hug. "Why didn't anybody tell me you'd be here too?"

"'Cause I didn't tell anybody. Decided to come to the men's breakfast last minute, ended up at Becky's move. Hey, Mom. How's that ankle?"

"Better. No crutches, see?" I wiggled my walking boot with the half sock over the toe.

"Hey, y'all!" Florida yelled from the front door. "Come on in here, get yourself warm. Carl should be back with the truck in two minutes, 'less he gets waylaid at Dunkin' Donuts."

We piled into the Hickmans' front room, where Florida had laid down newspapers and towels to soak up the slushy snow on our boots. Besides Carl Hickman and my husband and son, Ben Garfield and Peter Douglass had shown up too—a group of men

116

Florida and I had dubbed the "Bada-Boom Brothers" ever since they started meeting for prayer and support *before* the men's breakfast at SouledOut once a month. Ricardo Enriquez, Delores's husband, couldn't make it, but no surprise there. He drove for a trucking company, and his routes varied.

Carl Hickman came in just then, stamping his boots. "Hey, Carl," Denny said. "You going to pull the truck around to the alley, load from the back?"

Carl shook his head. "Nah. Outside steps are icy. Figured it'd be easiest to bring stuff down our inside stairs, but you gonna need to move your car so I can pull the truck closer to the house. Flo, where's Chris and Cedric? Didn't I tell those two we needed that walk shoveled?"

I left the men to figure out logistics and clumped slowly up the stairs to Becky's second-floor apartment at the back of the house. "I hope this girl knows what she's doin'," Florida mumbled, right on my tail. "Sure been nice havin' her an' Little Andy in that apartment—one of our own Yada Yada sisters, someone we don't have ta worry about."

I snickered; couldn't help it. "Yep. Ex-cons come highly recommended."

"Don't you be snickerin', Jodi Baxter. There but for the grace of God go a whole bunch of us—includin' you."

Ouch. That was the truth. I could have been given a prison sentence for vehicular manslaughter. Yo-Yo had done time, caught forging checks to feed and clothe her half brothers. Florida was an ex-drug addict . . . "Sorry, Flo. My comment was uncalled-for."

"Guess I have to forgive ya, 'cause you too big to wash your mouth out with soap—Chris! Cedric!" She pounded on her boys' bedroom doors as we passed. "Get your sorry behinds downstairs and get that walk shoveled!"

The door separating Becky Wallace's tiny apartment from the rest of the Hickman house stood open. "Hello!" I called. "Becky? What can I do to help? Where's Andy?"

Becky appeared in sweatshirt and sweatpants, flushed and bright-eyed. "Hey, Jodi. Uh . . . Stu and Estelle are over at the new place, cleaning. Yo-Yo's cleaning the bathroom. Little Andy's building a fort someplace downstairs with Carla—leastwise they stole half my blankets . . . Here." She handed me a roll of strapping tape. "Maybe you could tape up that stack of boxes over there."

I was glad to have something useful to do. Yo-Yo and I chatted as a clump of movers appeared and started carrying furniture down the stairs and out the front door. When it came time to move boxes, Carl organized everybody into a line to pass the boxes hand-to-hand down the stairs and out onto the porch; then he reorganized the line from the porch to the truck.

The truck was loaded before eleven-thirty.

Florida was everywhere at once, rounding up strays like an urban cowboy. "All right, everybody, take a break. We got some Popeye's chicken here an' some potato salad. Who's got Stu's cell phone number? Tell her and Estelle to get themselves over here for some lunch . . . "

I'd loaded my paper plate with a juicy chicken thigh and a mound of Florida's mustard potato salad when I realized Josh had disappeared. I'd just come out of the kitchen—he wasn't there. But his boots were still in the front hall. Curious, I slipped back up the stairs and made my way down the short hallway to Becky's empty apartment.

Josh was standing in the larger of the two rooms of the small studio, arms folded, turning slowly around in a 360.

"Josh?"

He looked my way. "Oh, hi, Mom. So that room"—he pointed toward the smaller room—"is the bedroom. Bathroom over there. And this room was—"

"Everything else." I grinned. "Kitchen, living room, sitting room. Becky had it fixed kinda cute, but it just got too small with Little Andy growing up."

"Uh-huh. And what are the Hickmans going to do with it now?"

"Well, they'd like to find another renter, but as you can see . . ."

A funny grin spread across my son's face. "I think they just found one."

13

*J*osh disappeared down the stairs, pulled Carl and Florida aside, and in two blinks the deal was done.

"Thank ya, *Je*sus!" Florida laughed like a giddy schoolgirl as she shut the front door behind the moving crew. "I been askin' God to bring someone to live in that oversize closet up there, but sure wasn't expectin' Him to drop the answer in our lap before the movin' truck even pulled away. Oh, Jesus! You are good, so good!"

I was still blinking. The sensation that events surrounding this wedding had just hit warp speed left me emotionally dizzy. "Well." I sat down on Florida's couch. "My goodness." I watched as Florida gathered up dirty towels from her front room floor. "That was quick."

"Ain't that just like God, Jodi? Oh, Jesus! Hallelujah." Florida burst into a couple of bars of "He's an On Time God," dancing around her living room with an armload of dirty towels.

"But if that tiny apartment was too small for Becky and Little

Andy, how's it going to be big enough for *three* people?" I shook my head. "Doesn't make sense."

"Now look here, Jodi Baxter. Don't you go questioning how God supplies a need. When Mary and Joseph got to Bethlehem, ridin' that donkey and her nine months pregnant—Lord, have mercy! Don't know how she did it!—I think they were downright grateful when God provided a stable. Now your son and his bride need a place right quick, somethin' they can afford. An' we just happen to have an empty apartment where they can move right in. *Humph.* Makes sense to me."

They needed something they could afford, all right. "Like . . . how much rent?"

Florida got right in my face. "*That* is none of your business. If your son wants to tell you, fine with me. But he's grown now, Jodi. He and Edesa are workin' things out—an' looks to me as if God is workin' things out too. Say, you mind pickin' up all them paper plates and napkins? I gotta get a trash bag for these towels so we can take 'em to the Laundromat later on." She disappeared into the kitchen.

Thank Me for My provision, Jodi.

I took a deep breath. *Right, Lord.* It wasn't up to me to work out all the details of this roller-coaster ride. I only had a walk-on part in this drama, but it was an essential one: *Don't worry . . . Trust God . . . Pray . . . Praise God for all His benefits.*

All His benefits. Like a washing machine.

"Hey, Flo!" I hollered, as I started picking up the paper trash scattered all over the compact living room. "Let me take those towels home and wash 'em, okay? You've got enough to do without a trip to the Laundromat. I'll bring them to church."

IF I THOUGHT the move was the biggest event of the day, I thought wrong. When Denny and Amanda picked me up at the Hickmans' after moving Becky into her new apartment, Amanda was bouncing all over the seat. "Mom! Estelle is going to make Edesa's dress for the wedding, and mine too! But we need to buy the material—is that okay? I mean, it'll be cheaper than going to Nordstrom or Lord & Taylor or someplace."

Lord & Taylor! Ha! Never in a zillion years had I even considered the possibility. Bless Estelle. "Um, sure, honey. Has Edesa got a pattern picked out?"

"No! That's what so neat. She said I could pick out a pattern I liked since she's only having one bridesmaid. But she'd like red material, since it's Christmas. Do you think red is my color?" Amanda prattled on, but it suddenly occurred to me that *I* was going to need a dress for this wedding too. The only thing I had in my closet remotely dressy was black and slinky. " . . . pick out the material today since she only has a week to work on it."

"Today?" *Of course today, you nincompoop. The wedding is next Saturday.* I tried not to panic. I'd been looking forward to getting off my feet for an hour, making a Christmas gift list, maybe doing some Christmas baking—not to mention I'd offered to wash Florida's towels, we still had to shop for groceries, and I had papers to grade. I needed two minutes to *think.*

"Yeah. Edesa and Delores are coming by to pick up Estelle and go to Vogue Fabrics in Evanston. Estelle said this would be the best time for you and me to go too."

Denny had zoned out of the conversation, intent on jockeying the minivan through the ice ruts in our alley and into the garage.

For a nanosecond, I was tempted to say, *"Oh, you go ahead."* Me, the martyr with the banged-up ankle.

I took a deep breath. Nope. My daughter was asking me to go along. God was in control, wasn't He? All things were going to work together for good . . . *Time for plan B, Jodi. Don't worry. Trust God. Pray. Praise.*

"Ah . . . okay. Tell you what. I need to get off this ankle for a while if we're going to go shopping. So I need you to wash these muddy towels for Florida—I promised to bring them back to her tomorrow." Denny, bless his heart, didn't know it yet, but he was going out again to do the grocery shopping.

"GUESS WHO CAME by while you were gone?" Denny said as I flopped onto the couch after our marathon shopping trip to Vogue Fabric.

"Can't guess," I moaned. "I'm exhausted. Put five women age eighteen to fifty-two in a fabric store, trying to choose a pattern and material for an opinionated teenage bridesmaid, while the bride and the 'mother of the bride' are arguing in Spanish half the time and . . . you get the idea."

"Who's fifty-two? You're only forty-six."

I closed my eyes, sinking deeper into the couch cushions. "Estelle," I murmured. "She's amazing. She cut through the non-sense . . . now she's got Edesa and Amanda upstairs taking mea-surements and fitting patterns." I opened one eye. "Who came by?"

"Hakim Porter."

"Hakim!" I rolled up on one elbow. "What did he want?"

"Asked if we wanted our walks shoveled again."

I vaguely remembered a shoveled walk when we returned from shopping, which is what it needed after yesterday's snowfall. I snickered and sank back on the cushions. "You sucker. You said yes. Did you get a chance to talk to him?"

Denny sat down on the hassock and leaned forward, elbows on his knees. "Not really. He seemed disappointed that you weren't here. Asked a couple of times if you were all right. But, funny thing, he was wearing shades . . ."

"Oh, you know, kids want to be cool."

"Maybe. But I don't think so. He seemed nervous, like he didn't want me to get too close to him. But when I gave him the money for shoveling the walks, I got a closer look . . . and I'm pretty sure he had a black eye and some bruises on his face."

"Oh no!" This time I sat up. "What happened? Did he say?"

Denny shook his head. "I asked, but he brushed it off. Disappeared pretty quick after that." He frowned, and then eyed me thoughtfully. "Any chance someone at his house is hitting him?"

"What? You mean his mother? No, no, I don't think she'd . . ." No, I couldn't imagine Geraldine Wilkins-Porter abusing her child. But then again, how well did I know the woman? She had had a lot of anger, true, but it had been directed at me—angry that her oldest child was dead, angry that the charges of vehicular manslaughter against me had been dropped. But Hakim? She was overly protective of him, if anything. At least she had been when he was in third grade.

"Oh, Denny, now I'm worried. What if some gangbangers beat him up? Or . . . I don't know. We need to pray for him."

Denny nodded, taking my extended hand. I could tell he was worried too.

THE HOUSE WAS still quiet when I schlepped into the living room in the blue half-light of early morning with the laundry basket of the Hickmans' clean towels. Shivering inside Denny's bathrobe, I plugged in the Christmas tree. Instantly, the multicolored lights bathed the room in quiet expectation. A childhood joy bubbled in my chest. It was beginning to look like Christmas.

Except there wasn't a single gift under the tree.

But the stable was there under the branches, with its wooden cow and donkey, and a tiny manger filled with bits of straw. Amanda had hidden baby Jesus until Mary and Joseph—currently "riding toward Bethlehem" along the windowsills—arrived on Christmas Eve. The shepherds and their assorted wooden sheep were already "abiding in the fields" on the coffee table; the three magi and their wooden camels, of course, had to start out in the dining room, the closest we came to a "far country."

It was a game Amanda and Josh had played ever since they were small, moving the nativity figures closer and closer to their destiny under the tree Christmas Eve.

I sat on the hassock, the room lit only by the Christmas tree lights, and pulled the laundry basket of clean towels within folding distance. Today was the last Sunday of Advent. Next Sunday was Christmas Day. Between now and then . . . *Ack!* I didn't even want to think about it.

Just enjoy the hush of this moment, Jodi, the Voice in my spirit seemed to say. *Carry that inner stillness with you into the coming week. Think about the old, old story which is ever new.*

I folded the Hickmans' towels, one by one, trying to meditate on the Christmas story. But I found myself thinking about Hakim, who just happened to show up on our doorstep unannounced, two and a half years after I'd been his third grade teacher. *Jesus, I don't understand why You brought Hakim back into my life right now. I mean, it's not as if he's the only one in the world who could shovel our walks. Why Hakim? Why now? A quirky coincidence? Or . . . did You send him for a reason? I'm worried about him, Lord. Please protect him. Don't let anyone hurt him.*

The Voice in my spirit was assuring. *Keep your eyes and your ears tuned to My Voice, Jodi. You'll understand the reason . . .*

I put the last folded towel back into the basket and reached for my Bible. I'd been reading Paul's letter to the Colossians in the New Testament ever since Avis quoted something from that book to encourage me a week or two ago. But now was as good a time as any to reread the Christmas story from Luke's Gospel.

The familiar words brought with them a flood of memories. The first time a youth group leader in our Bible church back in Des Moines, Iowa, had told us Mary was probably a teenager, maybe fifteen or sixteen, just like some of us, we were deliciously scandalized. Pregnant! No husband! No one believed her, of course. Not Joseph. Not her parents—

Huh. At the time, I always identified with poor, misunderstood Mary. But what about her parents? The Bible didn't say anything about her parents. But they must have been so disappointed. And then terrified. What if Joseph denounced their daughter's "unfaithfulness" and had her stoned? But he was a good man, who said he would just break off the engagement "quietly." And then, the next thing they knew, Joseph wanted a hurry-up wedding. He would take responsibility for the child as his own! Because (he said) an angel had told him in a dream not to be afraid.

Their parents must have thought they were crazy!

Just like me . . .

The Bible slipped from my lap. I stared at the stable, the humble birthplace of Jesus, under the tree. Joseph and Mary had put themselves on the line for a Baby who messed up all their plans—just like Josh and Edesa were doing for little Gracie. Even though their parents and others didn't understand. Even though there was "no room in the inn" for them . . .

It's time, Jodi, whispered the Voice in my spirit. *Time to make room in the inn of your heart for this hurry-up wedding and this unconventional child.*

14

I can't explain it. It was almost as if an angel had shown up in *my* living room and said, *"Don't be afraid. The child I'm giving to Edesa and Josh is God's child, and I've chosen them to be her parents."*

Nothing had changed . . . and yet a sweet joy started to bubble up within my spirit, tiny flutters of excitement reminiscent of the magic I used to feel as a child at Christmastime—except this was *real* Christmas, and the exhilaration was deeper and more urgent. I wanted to run . . . run like the shepherds and tell somebody, tell everybody, that what the angel said was true! God was alive among His people, working out His purpose—and I didn't need to be afraid!

Instead, I made a beeline for the kitchen phone as fast as my gimpy foot allowed, and dialed Josh's cell phone. It rang six times before he picked up. "Yeahumph?"

"Josh? Oh. Did I wake you?"

Two seconds of silence. "Mom. It's only, uh . . . 6:50."

"I'm sorry. Just wanted to tell you that you and Edesa are doing the right thing—going ahead with the wedding and the adoption, I mean. God told me it's all right."

Another brief silence. "Thanks, Mom. That means a lot. Really."

"School doesn't let out until Friday, which is a huge bummer! But if there's anything I can do . . . "

"I'm sure there'll be something, Mom. Just take care of yourself." I heard a click.

I hung up the phone sheepishly. "Huh. That was kind of dumb, waking him up just to tell him that," I murmured aloud, the way I used to do when Willie Wonka was underfoot. But I grinned. I didn't care. Back in the living room, I put on a CD of Christmas carols by the Brooklyn Tabernacle Choir, selected the funky Caribbean track I liked, and turned up the volume. *"Christ-mas! Christ-mas! First day of the Son . . . !"* Made me want to dance.

It was time for Denny and Amanda to get up anyway if we were going to get to church on time.

Not that they came out of their bedrooms singing and dancing. In fact, I got a bleary look from Amanda on her way to the bathroom, and a shout from Denny: "Jodi! Where's my bathrobe?"

I tossed Denny's robe into the bedroom and headed for the kitchen in my sleepshirt to make waffles. On my way through the dining room, I lit the fourth candle on our table Advent wreath and smiled. Well, let Denny and Amanda hear their own angel.

THE TEENS HAD decorated the sanctuary after the potluck last Sunday, and the room glowed. White lights outlined the large "storefront" windows, garlands of artificial greens and more lights adorned the walls, and a stunning banner in purple, red, and gold hung on the wall behind the low platform, proclaiming IMMANUEL! GOD WITH US ~ WONDERFUL COUNSELOR, MIGHTY GOD, EVERLASTING FATHER, PRINCE OF PEACE.

I drank it in, reflecting on each of the beautiful names of Jesus. But curiosity got the best of me. I said aloud to no one in particular, "Who made the beautiful banner?"

"Estelle Williams, I am told," said a familiar accent behind me.

The hairs on my neck stood up, as if someone had shuffled their feet across a carpet and zapped me with static. I whirled.

"Hoshi!" I screeched, throwing my arms around the tall, willowy young woman standing behind me. Then I held her at arm's length, drinking in the very sight of her. Hoshi Takahashi's jet-black hair hung long and silky down to her shoulders, softening her long face. Her bow-shaped smile pushed up her cheeks, turning her almond eyes into happy slits. "Hoshi Takahashi, you nearly gave me a heart attack! What are you doing here? When did you get back? You didn't tell us!"

"She told *me*." Peter Douglass leaned over Hoshi's shoulder and grinned. "I picked her up at O'Hare last night."

"So Avis . . . where's Avis! She knew, too, and didn't tell us?"

Peter moved off, chuckling.

"I am so happy to see you again, Jodi!" Hoshi took both of my hands in her long, slim ones. "I have missed Yada Yada so much. When I got Edesa's e-mail about the wedding, I could not wait." She glanced around the large room. "Will Josh and Edesa be here today?"

I giggled. "I don't know. I don't know anything! They're trying to plan a wedding . . . trying to move . . . trying to adopt . . . it's been a bit crazy around here."

I saw Florida and crew coming in the door, letting in a blast of frigid air, with Stu and Estelle right behind them and knew bedlam would break out when they saw Hoshi. I grabbed her in one last hug. "Oh, Hoshi, thank you so much for coming home."

THE ADVENT DANCERS that Sunday were even lovelier than before. Their dance was relaxed and lyrical, and I caught them glancing at Amanda, their dance coach, proud to show how well she had taught them. The lighting of a candle as we sang each verse of "O Come, O Come, Emmanuel" heightened the sense of expectation that had been building all month. And then the fourth candle was lit as we sang:

O come, Desire of nations, bind
All peoples in one heart and mind . . .

A promise yet to be fulfilled? It seemed like God had a long way to go to "bind all peoples" into one heart and mind. And yet— it *was* happening, in spite of governments and war and politics. Hoshi had come to us as a student from Japan . . . Edesa from Honduras . . . Nony had gone back to South Africa . . . I grew up in Iowa . . . Florida and Yo-Yo had been raised on the streets of Chicago . . . Delores's extended family was still in Mexico . . . Chanda had immigrated from Jamaica. Every one my sister because of Jesus. Jesus *had* made us one.

I was drained by the time the service was over. Even the scripture that morning from Isaiah 40 had rained like new words on my ears: "'Comfort, yes, comfort My people!' says your God . . . the crooked places shall be made straight, and the rough places smooth; the glory of the LORD shall be revealed, and all flesh shall see it together."

I still wasn't sure what had happened to me that morning. I couldn't begin to explain it to Denny, or to my Yada Yada sisters who swarmed all over Hoshi after the service, excited to meet at Avis's apartment that night and hear all about her months in Japan. All I knew is that the reality of *Immanuel*—*"God with us"* was not just something that happened two thousand years ago, but was still happening right now, in my life—me, Jodi Marie Baxter—and I felt comforted.

AVIS'S THIRD-FLOOR CONDO—she and Peter had moved into a lovely, red-brick building that had been renovated—felt like a secret hideaway tucked up among the treetops, although in winter only bare branches sheltered her exposed windows from the third-floor apartments across the street. But the gleaming wood floors, patterned area rugs, bookshelves, and tan-and-black leather furniture always invited me to unclutter my mind and drink in the calm.

However, Avis's apartment was anything but calm by the time all of us Yada Yadas crowded into the Douglass's living room that evening, talking all at once. Oh, wait. I didn't see Becky Wallace! When I asked Florida if she was coming, she shrugged. "Doesn't have a babysitter for Little Andy. Told that girl she shoulda stayed put." Oh dear. No car, no babysitter . . . surely she could figure out *something*.

Edesa showed up *without* Carmelita's baby. My soon-to-be daughter-in-law grinned at me. "Josh is babysitting. He might as well get used to changing diapers."

I giggled nervously. Hearing "Josh" and "changing diapers" in the same sentence was one more shock to my system. But I gave her a hug and whispered in her ear, the same message I had phoned to Josh early that morning. Her eyes teared up as she smiled and hugged me back.

With only a week until Christmas, the turnout for Yada Yada surprised me. Of course. Hoshi was back! Chatter swirled around her. Did she have a chance to talk to her parents again before she left? Did she think her aunt or younger sisters would come to Chicago to visit? When did her campus training begin? Where was she staying?

"She's staying with *us* for the moment," Avis broke in, coming into the room carrying a cake loaded with whipped cream and fruit. "This is a welcome-home treat, Hoshi. I hope I didn't massacre it too badly."

Hoshi's eyes widened when she saw the cake. "A Japanese Christmas cake!" She laughed when she saw the questions in our eyes. "Many Japanese celebrate Christmas, even though most are not Christians. But my family usually bought our Christmas cake."

The cake was a marvel, like a sponge cake with strawberries, blueberries, raspberries, and peaches not only on top but in the middle. Where Avis found fresh berries in Chicago in December was beyond me. Florida poked me as Avis cut the cake. "Didn't know Avis could make anythang 'cept mac 'n cheese," she murmured.

I snickered. "You're so bad, Flo."

Avis finally managed to call us together by beginning our

prayer time with the chorus to "O Come, All Ye Faithful." We all joined in the slow, worshipful words: *"O come, let us adore Him, O come, let us adore Him, O come, let us adore Hi-im, Chri-ist, the Lord."* As the chorus ended, Avis rephrased the words and we kept singing: *"For He alone is worthy, for He alone is worthy, for He alone is worthy-y, Chri-ist the Lord."*

After worship, Hoshi shared more about her plans to join International Student Outreach on American campuses, starting with her training in January. "But I am so happy to have a few weeks just to be with Yada Yada, my first spiritual family. Although, I was hoping Nonyameko would be here. Is she not coming after all?"

"Yes! She's coming!" several of us chorused, although I was worried. We still hadn't heard when, exactly, the Sisulu-Smiths were arriving.

"Dat sista *better* come home!" Chanda folded her arms. "'Cause we planning a big reunion party on de New Year, an' mi already bought a dress an' shoes."

"But that was before we knew Edesa was gettin' married," Yo-Yo protested. "I don't want to get dressed up *twice* in the same week—"

The whole room hooted and burst into laughter. The most any of us had seen Yo-Yo "dressed up" was a new pair of overalls at Avis's wedding.

"—unless I can wear my overalls to—"

"No!" five voices cried at once.

"Not to de wedding, Yo-Yo Spencer." Now it was Chanda's turn to protest. "Dis time we *all* gettin' decked out for dis wedding, an dat means you, too, sista girl."

135

"But it's just at the shelter."

"All de more reason," Chanda sniffed. "Mi want me t'ree kids to show some respect for a wedding, even if it's not in de church."

"Kids, schmids." Ruth rolled her eyes. "A wedding we're having with babies, kids, husbands, *oy vey!* Maybe the reunion should be just Yada Yada." She fanned herself.

"Perdóneme!" Edesa squeaked. She looked on the verge of tears. "I did not want our wedding to upset plans for the reunion. We chose Christmas weekend because we knew Yada Yada's reunion was scheduled for New Year's, so Nony could be here . . . "

My heart melted. Ever since Josh and Edesa had announced their intentions, I'd been fussing about the date, wondering why they didn't wait until after Christmas—and all the time, Edesa had been willing to sacrifice the more reasonable time, even sacrifice Nony and Mark's presence, so it wouldn't conflict with our reunion.

I confessed, right then and there, and asked Edesa to forgive me. Now Edesa really was crying, and we hugged and rocked a long time.

"Ahem!" Adele cleared her throat, arms across her bosom. "I think we should appoint a reunion committee to make plans, tell us what's going to happen, and the rest of us will show up. And leave Edesa and Jodi off the committee—they have enough to do with the wedding coming first."

"Leave me off too!" Estelle rolled her eyes. "I have a wedding dress to make!"

Adele's suggestion met cheers and applause. In quick succession, Adele, Stu, and Chanda volunteered—and Avis was shanghaied.

We closed the meeting with prayers of praise for bringing

Hoshi back to us and then gathered around Edesa, laying hands on her and blessing this huge leap in her life, from single student to mother and wife. *And daughter-in-law,* I thought.

As the prayers ended, Stu asked Edesa, "Are you registered for wedding gifts? What do you need?"

"Registered?" Edesa looked confused. Stu explained about registering at her favorite stores so people could get gifts she wanted and needed.

Edesa laughed. "We need everything! But especially things for the baby."

"Everything?" Ruth snorted. "If it's everything you need, then it's everything you've got. You can have it all—changing table, diaper pail, baby swing, baby clothes. In fact, get pregnant on your wedding night if you want—we have doubles! But it'll have to be a *boytshik.*"

15

I choked. Edesa squirmed. Everybody else laughed.

Good grief. That was my son's sex life Ruth was talking about! Of course, I supposed it *could* happen . . . *Ack!* No, wasn't going to go there. I had too many other things to think about this week. Like five full days of school bumping right up against Christmas Eve. Like finding a dress to wear to my son's wedding. Like seeing that Josh and Edesa got moved in with the necessities to set up housekeeping. Not to mention Christmas shopping and a wedding gift . . .

Josh called Monday while we were eating supper to ask if he could borrow our minivan to move his stuff into the Hickmans' studio apartment. "Then I can stay there until Saturday morning, when we can move Edesa's stuff."

"Sure. I can help," Denny said. "What time's the wedding again?"

I had picked up the bedroom extension, and was glad Denny asked. Had they ever given us an actual time?

"Five o'clock. But we're doing a Christmas party for the kids at the shelter at one. Hopefully that'll give enough time to clean up from the party and decorate for the wedding."

A Christmas party for the shelter kids *before* the wedding?! I stuffed my face into a pillow to keep from telling him they were out-and-out, absolutely, totally and completely crazy!

"Mom? You still on the phone?"

I untangled from the pillow. "Um, right here."

"Remember you asked if there was anything you could do to help? Well, we thought of something. A huge favor, actually. Chanda George gave us two nights at the Orrington Hotel in Evanston for a wedding gift. So we're wondering if you'd be willing to take Gracie after the wedding. We'd come back for a while on Christmas Day, eat Christmas dinner with you guys, hang out for a while, then go back to the hotel . . . "

My mind scrambled. *Take care of a baby? For a whole weekend?* How long had it been! I didn't know anything about Gracie's schedule, if she slept through the night, or anything. "Uh, two nights at the Orrington! What a nice wedding gift from Chanda."

"Yeah. But about Gracie . . . "

I took a deep breath. "Of course, Josh. That's a great idea, for you and Edesa to have a honeymoon weekend. I'd be happy to do that." *God, please make that be true.*

"About Christmas, though. Edesa and I don't have time or money right now to do Christmas shopping, for obvious reasons. What if we Baxters don't exchange Christmas gifts this year? Maybe just stocking stuffers; that'd be fun. Besides, you taking care of Gracie for us Christmas Eve will be a huge gift to us."

"Makes sense," I heard Denny say. "We haven't been able to do much either since your mom got her wings clipped by that fall. If you two actually show up for Christmas dinner the day after your wedding"—he chuckled—"we'll consider that your gift to us."

I should've felt disappointment. No gifts under the tree? But instead, relief eased itself into my spirit and put its feet up. Wouldn't it be wonderful not to have to go shopping? Well, except for a dress to wear to the wedding, and some practical wedding gifts. But besides that, it felt . . . right. More time to spend together. More time to reflect on the manger under the tree . . .

Huh. Who do I think I'm kidding? I'll be lucky to slide into that wedding like a bobsledder.

"Oh, one more thing," Josh was saying. "I invited the grandparents—and I think they're both coming. Harley and Kay said not to worry about them. They'll fly in and get a hotel. But Grandma and Grandpa Jennings will need a place to stay. I told them they could have my bed at your house. Hope that's okay."

HARLEY AND KAY. Denny's New York, "call us by our first name" parents were the epitome of retirees happily spending their children's inheritance, traveling to Europe for six weeks every year, plus taking a cruise to Alaska or the Caribbean or some other exotic port. I was surprised they were even in the country.

My parents, on the other hand, were stay-at-home "Grandpa and Grandma" folks with limited income. They'd had a year and a half to get used to the idea that Josh's fiancée was not only Honduran but black. They'd privately expressed a few worries about a "mixed marriage" and "what about the children?" But when they'd met Edesa at Amanda's high school graduation, they'd

141

immediately fallen in love with her. "She's a real Christian," my dad had said.

But it blessed my socks right off that they would make the six-hour drive from Des Moines to Chicago in the dead of winter. I prayed all week for no snow, even though my students were probably praying for a white Christmas. The temperatures hovered close to zero, and for once I was glad. Too cold to snow. It warmed up Thursday and we got several new inches—but Friday's temperatures hiked into the forties and melted it all.

Thank You, Jesus!

By the time I got home from school on Friday—walking on my own two feet, though I still wore an elastic bandage around my left ankle—my folks were upstairs with Amanda at Stu and Estelle's apartment, drinking coffee, inhaling Stu's infamous cranberry bread, and oohing and aahing over the nearly finished wedding gown and Amanda's red bridesmaid's dress. My mother's cheeks were pink, and my dad—his dome shinier and his shoulders more stooped than the last time I saw them—had a twinkle in his eyes.

The party had begun.

I'd given up on finding a dress to wear to the wedding and had decided to go with Stu's suggestion to accessorize my slinky black dress. But that evening my mother pulled me aside. "I know you said we aren't exchanging gifts this Christmas, honey. But . . . I thought you might enjoy having this." She thrust a package at me. "It was your grandmother's."

"Oh, Mom." I opened the tissue paper. Inside was a cream-colored, lacy shawl, hand-crocheted out of silky thread. Pale pink roses and swirls had been crocheted into the delicate pattern. A long silky fringe hung from each end. It would go perfectly with my slinky black dress and Stu's zircon bracelet, necklace, and dangle earrings. "Oh, Mom, I love it. Thank you so much." But even as we hugged, I knew what it was. *God's provision.*

DENNY TOOK THE minivan Saturday morning to help Josh move Edesa's clothes and other belongings to their new home. "You should see this apartment, Dad," I giggled, serving a streusel coffee cake for breakfast, hot and dripping with brown sugar, butter, and cinnamon in honor of their visit. "Just don't call it a hole-in-the-wall—even if it is. The baby has more furniture in there than they do. At least someone gave Josh and Edesa a queen-size mattress and box springs, though right now the bed's on the floor."

Right after breakfast, my dad got the turkey ready to pop into the oven the next day for Christmas dinner, while my mom and I made pies and cut up bread and onions for stuffing. By twelve noon, we were in my parents' car heading for Manna House, where we'd agreed to meet Denny, give the grandparents a tour of the shelter, take in the Christmas party, and help any way we could with wedding preparations.

Estelle was still putting final touches on the dresses and said she'd bring them later, in time to help Edesa and Amanda dress. I brought a garment bag with Denny's suit and my dress, figuring jeans were more appropriate for a kids' Christmas party anyway.

"Grandpa! Grandma!" Josh said, bounding across the multipurpose room and enveloping his grandparents in one big hug. "Edesa! Look who's here!"

Edesa, wearing jeans and a sweatshirt, with her thick, kinky-curly hair bunched into a ponytail at the nape of her neck, looked up from the knot of kids hanging on her and broke into a wide smile. She ran over and gave each of my parents a warm hug and kiss. "*Abuela y Abuelo,* you have come! *Muchas gracias.*"

"What did she say?" my dad murmured.

Josh laughed. "She called you Grandmother and Grandfather." He looked around. "Edesa, where's Gracie? I want my grandparents to meet her."

Four-month-old Gracie was nodding off over the shoulder of one of the shelter residents, but Edesa reclaimed her to show her off. All around us, residents and staff bustled about, setting up chairs, shooing the children downstairs to the recreation room, hanging up last-minute tinsel garlands, and bringing up a punch bowl and plates of Christmas cookies from the kitchen downstairs.

As my parents chuckled and cooed at the baby, I wandered over to the Christmas tree in the corner and fingered the branches. *Artificial.* I grinned. Good for Manna House. The tree looked real enough, covered with multicolored minilights, handmade snowflakes, paper chains, and salt dough decorations—probably made by the children of the Katrina refugees, most of whom were still waiting for more permanent placement.

I stepped back. Odd. There were no gifts under the tree. For a kids' Christmas party? It was one thing for the Baxters to forgo Christmas gifts this year, but *these* kids—

"Don't worry, Mom." Josh's voice murmured in my ear. He must have read my mind—or my body language. "Weiss Memorial adopted our shelter as their Christmas project this year. Some of their staff and volunteers are bringing gifts for the party. But I asked them to show up at one-thirty, *after* our little Christmas program, so as not to distract the kids. Now . . . could you and Dad give the grandparents a tour of Manna House or something so Edesa and I can finish rehearsing our little pageant with the kids? We're still trying to clean up some of their language, like—"

"I get it, I get it. I teach third graders, remember?"

I rounded up Denny and my parents and took them on a tour of the new facility, dodging assorted children running up and down the stairs, all the while thinking maybe it was a blessing my parents were getting hard of hearing.

By the time we got back to the multipurpose room, the chairs were filling up with shelter residents, staff, and volunteers. *Volunteers* . . . I hadn't given much thought to Rev. Handley's invitation at the dedication. Then again, I hadn't had much time to think about *anything* in the last five weeks! I really did need a vacation or a retreat or someth—

Someone grabbed me from behind in a bear hug. I wiggled around. "Precious McGill! I was hoping I'd see you!" The former shelter resident who'd come to stay at our house after the fire beamed at me from beneath a head full of tiny braids. "Precious, this is my mom and dad—"

Precious pumped their hands. "Well, now, that's right nice! Ain't this the bomb? Oh, gotta go. They ready to start, an' we first on the program."

I had no idea what "first on the program" meant, but I soon found out. A choir of about nine youngsters—mostly girls, but two self-conscious boys—gathered in front of the rows of chairs and sang "Mary Had a Baby," with Precious as choir director. I was amazed at the sound she drew from those kids—most of whom were not only homeless but had been traumatized by the Katrina Hurricane. *"She named Him King Jesus, yes, Lord . . . people keep a-comin' an' the train done gone . . . "* The song was soulful, a mixture of hope and pathos.

Then a little African-American girl around age six or seven, with five fat braids sectioning her hair, stood front and center while Precious put a CD in a boom box and turned up the volume. In a sweet voice, the little girl began to sing: "Happy Birthday, Jesus"—a song I recognized from the Brooklyn Tabernacle Christmas CD. I saw a smile begin on my father's face as he listened, and then grow wider as the child sang. *". . . and the presents are nice, but the real gift is You . . . "*

The little choir ended with a side-swaying, hand-clapping "Go Tell It on the Mountain," bringing most of us out of our seats, swaying and clapping along. I could tell my parents were enjoying themselves.

As the choir scattered, the "Christmas pageant" began . . . with a teenage Mary startled by a ten-year-old angel wrapped in a sheet. "You're gonna get pregnant, and it was the Holy Ghost who did it!"

Kids giggled and the adults tried to stifle their laughter as the "angel" appeared to a teenage Joseph and told him to quit messing around and marry Mary. The "trip to Bethlehem" around the multi-purpose room resulted in Mary and Joseph getting told at the Christmas tree, the couch, and the refreshment table: "Sorry. Don't got no room." A box filled with towels served as the "manger," in which a very much alive baby Gracie kicked and fussed, setting off a sweet "Aww" around the whole room.

Finally, the "angel" found a bunch of "shepherds" in a far corner and told them: "I've got great news! Jesus is born—and you'll find Him in a barn." The "shepherds" in bathrobes and bath-towel turbans ran full tilt and skidded to a stop beside the box with the baby, grinning and giggling.

As the audience clapped and the children took their bows, suddenly my throat tightened and my eyes watered. *How utterly appropriate to see the Christmas story here in this homeless shelter. An ordinary teenage Mary, a working-class Joseph, a bunch of "shepherds" who in today's world might have been auto-shop mechanics. When Jesus was born, angels had to announce it because it happened right under everyone's noses; so humble and ordinary, most people missed it. People still missed it—*

A commotion at the back interrupted my thoughts. Heads turned; a number of adults and a few children in winter coats wearing "Santa's elves" caps swept in through the double doors carrying bags and boxes of gaily wrapped Christmas gifts. The shelter kids cheered and started a mad scramble.

"Hey! Hey!" Josh grabbed a few shirts and pulled them back. "Come on now, all you kids sit on the floor around the tree . . . that's right. These good folks are from Weiss Memorial Hospital, and they've brought gifts for everyone. Come on, let's show some appreciation!" Josh led the clapping as Precious and others took the coats of the Weiss Memorial elves and helped them put the gifts under the tree for distribution.

As one of the women put her load of gifts under the tree and straightened, I squinted and stared. The woman looked familiar, someone I knew or had seen before—and then I saw the boy with her.

Hakim Porter! With his mother, Geraldine Wilkins-Porter.

They were standing off to the side, watching as Josh and Edesa read the nametags on the gifts and handed them out, when I approached. "Mrs. Porter?"

Hakim's mother turned. The African-American woman—I vaguely remembered she worked as a licensed practical nurse—looked as slim and professional as the last painful time I'd seen her in my classroom at Bethune Elementary, when our hands had briefly touched, somewhat easing the tension between us, though she had been unable to forgive me. Now, recognition twitched at the corners of her eyes. Her lips parted slightly.

"Mrs. Baxter. I didn't realize . . . " She seemed confused about why I was at a women's shelter.

I smiled, trying to put her at ease. "My son is on the advisory board here." I decided not to mention the upcoming wedding in a few hours. Too complicated. But should I tell her Hakim had been to our house recently and shoveled our walks? I glanced at the boy, standing just behind his mother and nearly as tall, and caught his worried eyes and urgent shake of the head. So I just held out my hand. "Hello, Hakim. It's wonderful to see you again."

He shook my hand, then faded from sight.

"Well . . . Merry Christmas. We can't stay long." Geraldine Porter turned as if ending the conversation. "Boomer?" The woman frowned. "Now, where did that boy go? I told him not to go running off! He's always disappearing on me."

Boomer? My mouth went dry. I licked my lips. In my mind I felt the jerk again that sent me sprawling, saw the shadowy figure who'd come back, heard the distant voice yelling, *"Boomer, you idiot! Get outta there!"*

16

*B*oom . . . Boomer?" I hoped my voice didn't squeak.

Mrs. Porter looked at me quizzically, as if she'd already forgotten I was there. "Oh. Just a nickname. He used to have a boom box he carried everywhere, like an extra appendage. His cousins started calling him Boomer. Now they have me saying it." She swiveled her head. "Excuse me, I need to find him."

I stood rooted in the same spot, my thoughts and feelings spinning. It all fell into place, like twisting a Rubik's Cube one last time and suddenly all the colors matched. *Hakim* had been with the teens who had stolen my purse and knocked me down. It was Hakim who had come back to help me, had found my phone, had dialed 9-1-1. Someone had yelled, called him *"Boomer,"* and told him to run.

Across the room, Geraldine Wilkins-Porter and her son retrieved their coats and headed out the double doors. At the last moment, Hakim turned, caught my eye, and lifted his hand in good-bye. I waved back weakly.

I sank into the closest chair. It must have been Hakim who had returned my stolen purse and credit cards. But . . . why?

Stupid question. Because he feels guilty. He's sorry but can't say it, can't admit he was part of what happened.

The party was basically over. The Manna House staff must have sent the names of each child to Weiss Memorial with a wish list, because all the children seemed delighted with their gifts. I pushed myself out of the chair to help with cleanup. *Lord, this can't just be coincidence!—even Hakim and his mother showing up today. But what's it all about? I'd like to tell him I forgive him, but . . . I don't even know where he lives. And his mom obviously doesn't know he's been showing up to shovel our walks. Lord, I don't know what You want to happen, but please, at least bring Hakim back to our house once more. Give us some time to talk . . .*

THE SHELTER SWIRLED with activity as laughing residents helped transform the multipurpose room into a "chapel" for the wedding. No baskets of flowers—too expensive, Josh said—but two iron candelabras Edesa had borrowed from *Iglesia del Espirito Santo* stood at the front of the rows of folding chairs, each holding five long white tapers and decorated with wide red bows.

Delores Enriquez, the honorary mother of the bride, showed up with her entire family at two-thirty and immediately took charge of coordinating wedding setup and details. I was delighted to see her husband, Ricardo, show up with his large *guitarron*. Ricardo had a way of coaxing love from his big guitar—perfect for a wedding.

José, Delores's oldest, seemed as if he'd grown six inches since I last saw him at Lane Tech's graduation last spring. A first-year student at UIC, he was as tall as his father, maybe five-seven, although he seemed taller because of his slender build. Amanda screeched with delight when she saw him, throwing her arms around his neck and then babbling like an auctioneer as the two "just friends" caught up on the months they'd been at different colleges.

My mom offered to stay with Gracie when Edesa put the baby down for a nap in the portable crib in Edesa's stripped-down room. Most of their things had already been taken to the "Hickman Hilton," as I heard Denny refer to it. "Smart move," I teased my mom. "Way to sneak in a nap too."

Stu and Estelle arrived with the dresses—hidden in garment bags, of course. A parade of jean-clad Yada Yada sisters turned up with food, garment bags, and wedding gifts. Yo-Yo and the Garfields arrived with the wedding cake from the Bagel Bakery. After helping to set up chairs, I zipped downstairs to the dining room where the reception would be held to take a peek, but decided not to tangle with Ruth, who was insisting that the cake table had to be moved. "A place of honor it must be. No, no, not there—here!"

On my way back up the stairs to the main floor, I passed Emerald, Delores's next oldest, as she shepherded her three younger siblings toward the rec room on the lower floor. "Oh, *Señora* Baxter!" The girl's eyes danced, her long hair a cascade of dark waves falling behind the red ribbon she wore. "My *quinceañera* is this spring! Will you come?"

What? She's fifteen already? Impossible . . . "Of course, Emerald.

You will be a beautiful *Quinceañera*." I gave her a hug. "Who is going to be your escort?" Emerald giggled and shrugged. I watched her disappear.

It seemed only yesterday that the Enriquez family—José especially—had spearheaded a *quinceañera*, the traditional Mexican coming-of-age party, for our Amanda. I was grateful José and Amanda had survived their first teenage love and breakup and been able to remain friends—though even my heart had skipped a beat when José came in, no longer a boy but a dark-eyed, handsome hunk.

"Jodi!" Delores cornered me as I came back into the multipurpose room. "Did Josh or Edesa speak to you about reading the scripture during the service?"

I shook my head. "Nope. You know what they say about the mother of the groom: 'Wear beige and stand in a corner.'"

She looked into my eyes, reading my heart. "Be patient, Jodi. They've only had two weeks to put this wedding together. They would like you to read the scripture—Colossians 3, verses 12 through 14. Do you have your Bible?"

I shook my head. "No, I wasn't expecting . . ."

She smiled. "No problem. Reverend Handley let me borrow hers, just in case." She handed me a worn brown leather Bible with *Elizabeth Handley* engraved on the front in gold scroll letters. "And here's the order of service. You can see when the scripture reading comes. Peter Douglass printed it at his shop. Isn't it beautiful?"

The folded program on creamy, watermarked paper was indeed beautiful. A swell of gratefulness drowned my momentary crabbiness. *Thank You, Jesus, for all our "brothers and sisters" who are doing so much to make this hasty wedding a beautiful moment in time.*

I looked at my watch. Three-thirty. Maybe I could disappear for a while to practice reading the scripture and get myself dressed before helping Amanda. Some peace and quiet, some prayer and Scripture, sounded like just what Dr. Jesus ordered for my sweating palms.

Josh—my oldest child, my only son—was getting married in less than two hours.

I HAD FINISHED dressing and was hooking Stu's earrings into my earlobes when Denny, still in his jeans and sweatshirt, peeked into the bunkroom I'd been using. "Jodi? I think you need to come out here." His words suggested alarm, but not his grin.

"What?"

"Just come!" He grabbed me by the hand and pulled me down the stairs to the main floor. As we neared the multipurpose room, I heard squeals and a babble of excited voices. At the doorway, Denny stepped back and pushed me forward.

On the other side of the room, an animated swarm was milling at the back of the rows of chairs, mostly my Yada Yada sisters, laughing, squealing, hugging. I saw Josh pumping the hand of someone, an African-American man in a dark suit . . . and then I saw the black-and-gold African head wrap next to him, the gracious tilt of the head, the wide smile framed by the rich color of dark oak.

Astonishment sucked the breath right out of my body. *Nonyameko and Mark!* Two seconds later, I was pushing my way into the knot of bodies around the Sisulu-Smith family. I reached for Nony, who was laughing and trying to hug everyone at once.

"You're here! You're here! I thought—oh! Oh! This is wonderful!" I hugged Nony, hugged Mark—oh! That beautiful man, still wearing an eye patch, but otherwise looking fit and handsome, still sporting an elegant goatee—and then hugged their two young teens, Marcus and Michael, who were wearing black dashikis embroidered in white and seemed a bit uncomfortable with all the fuss.

"Oh, man, Dr. Smith," I heard Josh say. "If I'd known you were going to be here in time for the wedding, I would have asked you to stand up with me or something."

Mark Smith laughed. "Not a good idea, son. I might topple over from jet lag. It is enough that we can be here to witness this magnificent event."

"Oh, Nony." My eyes were tearing up. "We thought . . . I mean, weren't you going to spend Christmas with your family in Durban? How did you . . . I mean—"

Nonyameko wrapped her arms around me. I could smell the soft fabric of her flowing tunic, the warm musk of her skin. "Oh, Jodi. When we got Edesa's e-mail, that she and your Josh were getting married on Christmas Eve, we could not stay away. We did not tell anyone because we were not sure we could change our tickets and we did not want to disappoint. Holiday travel, you know. But . . . " Her smile warmed me all over. "God made all the rough places smooth. Here we are."

I was so happy I could hardly speak. Everyone was here. My Yada Yada sisters had come home because they loved Edesa and my son.

Nony looked around. "Where is Edesa?" I realized Amanda and Estelle were missing too.

"She is getting dressed," Delores said, "which is what you should be doing as well, Joshua Baxter." She looked disapprovingly at the array of jeans and sweats. "The rest of you too—shoo, shoo! Get dressed."

The Yada Yadas dispersed reluctantly, but the room definitely was quiet after they disappeared upstairs to the bunkrooms to dress. I realized Denny's parents had also arrived while I'd been dressing and were talking to my parents, who were sitting on a couch in a corner of the room. My father was holding little Gracie, dressed in a frilly white outfit I suspected came from Delores's children. I slipped over to greet the senior Baxters, letting Nony and Mark slip away to greet Ben Garfield, who was riding herd on his two-year-old twins.

"Jodi, dear." Kay Baxter, her silver-blonde hair cut short and sassy, kissed me on both cheeks, something she probably picked up in France. "You're looking well. Didn't you break your leg or something?" Her eyes took in the multipurpose-room-turned-chapel. "This is all rather sweet. But surely there is a church *somewhere* they could have used in a safer part of town? I wasn't sure I wanted to get out of the taxi!"

Oh, brother. Sometimes I wondered how this couple had given birth to my Denny.

Denny's father rolled his eyes. "Kay, sweetheart, it was perfectly fine. So, this is the baby?" he said to my father. "She's a pretty little thing, isn't she?"

The baby . . . I had hardly had any time to think about Gracie the past few days or the fact that I had agreed to take care of her after the wedding. *Oh God, I feel pulled in too many directions!*

Well, let the grandparents fuss over her for now. My time would come.

155

I politely chatted with both sets of grandparents until Denny showed up in his black dress suit, white shirt, and a red tie. Ricardo Enriquez began to play his solo guitar; our voices lowered to whispers. Peter Douglass and Carl Hickman acted as ushers, greeting people as they came in, giving out programs, and seating those who needed help. Peter Douglass beckoned our family group, seating the four grandparents and Gracie into the second row on the "groom's side," then steering me to a seat in the front row.

But Denny didn't sit down. "Where are you going?" I whispered.

My husband grinned, his dimples going deep. "I'm going to escort the bride."

I shook my head, laughing silently. Actually, it was kind of fun not knowing all the plans for the wedding. Surprise after surprise.

The room filled. Katrina evacuees and shelter residents, dressed in the best clothes they could manage under the circumstances—which in some cases meant clean jeans and T-shirts—filled half the seats. Our Yada Yada Prayer Group and their families were sprinkled on both sides of the aisle. At the last moment, Delores Enriquez hustled up the aisle with her three youngest children in tow, handed a bulging diaper bag and bottle to Gracie's caretakers behind me, and sat in the front row on the "bride's side." We glanced at each other and grinned. "Our" children were getting married.

17

s Ricardo launched into a medley of Christmas carols on his guitar, Emerald Enriquez walked down the aisle carrying a lit candle, wearing a simple white dress with a red sash and . . . red heels. *Oh my. She really is growing up!* After lighting all the candles on both of the iron candelabras, Emerald joined her mother and siblings on the front row . . . and on cue, three men walked in solemnly from the door off to the side. I smiled. Their only similarity was that each carried a Bible and was wearing a suit.

I felt a poke from behind. "Who are *they*?" Kay Baxter whispered.

"The man on the left is Pastor Rodriquez," I whispered over my shoulder, "Edesa's pastor, from *Iglesia del Espirito Santo*. The other two are our pastors from SouledOut Community Church—Pastor Clark and Pastor Cobbs." My soul wanted to sing—or at least giggle with pleasure. A Latino pastor, a white pastor, and an African-

American pastor, all on the same platform (although there was no platform). Josh and Edesa had brought them together—had brought all of us together—in this place and on this day.

Florida must have been thinking the same thing. From two rows back, I heard her stage whisper. "Now ain't that a picture of what it's goin' ta be like at the Marriage Feast of the Lamb! Know what I'm sayin'?"

The side door opened again, and Josh walked in, followed by José. I had a twinge of familiar "labor panic": *This is it! There's no turning back!* I blew out a deep breath and found a smile. Josh, his sandy hair trimmed up for his wedding, wore a black suit, open-necked white shirt, and a red vest. José, dark-eyed and dark-haired, wore a similar black suit, open-necked shirt, and red vest. Unrelated thoughts bumped in my head: *How in the world did Estelle manage to make vests too?* And . . . *Wow. Gotta admit, both young men are drop-jaw handsome.*

As if by instinct, heads turned. Amanda walked slowly down the aisle in time to the sweet guitar music. Her honey-colored hair was piled on her head, with curls and tendrils mixed with skinny red and white ribbons. *Adele must have been busy in the back room,* I thought. The simple red dress rippled like water as she walked. She carried a single long-stemmed white rose. I heard murmuring around me . . . *"Lovely."* But what I *saw* was the wink José sent her way.

And then the guitar thrummed like a stringed drumroll . . . and Ricardo began to play the traditional wedding march. Everyone stood and looked toward the back of the room where the double doors opened into the foyer. Edesa stood in the open doorway, one hand holding Denny's arm, the other a single long-stemmed red rose. A sigh rippled through the room. The white dress she wore, hanging in simple lines to the floor, included a short bolero jacket with long sleeves. But the stunning touch was a lace *mantilla* draped over Edesa's dark hair and flowing to the floor.

Delores caught my eye, smiled, and pointed to herself. *"My wedding mantilla,"* she mouthed silently.

At the front, Denny kissed the bride's cheek, then joined me on the front row as Edesa took Josh's arm. The music stopped and Pastor Rodriquez stepped forward. I could no longer see Josh's face, but it seemed to me he couldn't keep his eyes off Edesa. I clutched Denny's hand.

"Bienvenidos! Welcome!" Pastor Rodriquez boomed. "Today we have the joy of uniting two young people in holy matrimony . . . "

The simple ceremony seemed to pass in a blur. The next thing I knew, Pastor Joseph Cobbs, in his rich bass voice, was asking Josh and Edesa to repeat their vows. Pastor Clark, a bit more shrunken these days inside his loose-fitting suit, did the vows with the wedding rings. "I'm so glad they included him," I whispered to Denny.

Denny pointed to the program. "You're on next."

Sure enough, after the rings Pastor Rodriquez said, "The scripture Josh and Edesa have chosen will be read by *Señora* Baxter." He smiled and beckoned. *"Señora?"*

Grateful for the elegant shawl my mother had given me, I joined the wedding party at the front and turned to the place I'd marked in my Bible. "I'm reading from Colossians chapter 3, verses 12 through 14." I cleared my throat. "'Therefore, as God's chosen people, holy and dearly loved, clothe yourselves with compassion, kindness, humility, gentleness and patience—'"

I caught my breath. The words *"clothe yourselves"* stuck in my ears. I almost gasped in amusement, remembering our lively Yada Yada discussion last week about coming "decked out" to Josh and Edesa's wedding. And not one minute ago, I was preening in the antique shawl that dressed me up and made me "presentable" for a wedding. But this scripture was talking about being "decked out" with compassion! Kindness! Humility!

Hoping I hadn't paused too long, I hastened to the next verse. "'Bear with each other and forgive whatever grievances you may have against one another. Forgive as the Lord forgave you. And over all these virtues put on love—'"

At that moment, Gracie sent up a loud wail. Delores sprang from her seat, as if she was going to take the baby out, but Josh said, "No, no, it's okay." Grinning, he moved toward the second row and collected Gracie from my mother. Then, shushing the baby, he returned to Edesa's side. The three of them turned slightly to face me. Smiles and murmurs danced along the rows of wedding guests as Gracie looked wide-eyed into Josh's face, hiccoughed once, and then banged his nose with her waving fist.

I stared at my son, his new bride, and the baby that wasn't his or hers, but that they were hoping to make their own. I suddenly saw them, and the scene around me, as if cataracts had just been peeled from my eyes. I closed my Bible, but heard myself saying, "May I say something?"

Pastor Rodriquez smiled. *"Por favor."*

Oh Lord, am I crazy? Please give me the words to say what is in my heart!

I took a deep breath. "I'm sure many of us, myself included, thought having a wedding in a women's shelter was a bit, um, unusual." I heard a few snickers of agreement. "And the wedding date was hurried up because Edesa and Josh want to provide a home for little Gracie, here. So here we are, on Christmas Eve, and as I read these verses, I'm suddenly realizing how utterly appropriate for this wedding to take place on this day, in this place—"

"Say it now, girl!" Florida called out.

I smiled, gaining courage. "—because God chose humble circumstances and a hurry-up wedding to make a home for His Son. He chose the humble to receive Him . . ." I suddenly choked up, and Denny had to step up and hand me his handkerchief. I blew my nose and dabbed my eyes, hoping I wasn't smearing my mascara. "Sorry."

"That's all right," Adele said from the back. "Take your time."

I saw Denny's parents exchange a look, but I didn't care.

"Anyway, all I want to say is that the Christ Child was God *incarnate*—God's love made *real*. And . . . and it seems to me what we are witnessing today is that same kind of incarnated love—love made real, love in action and not just words." I turned my eyes on Josh and Edesa, who were looking a little teary themselves. "Josh and Edesa, you both look so beautiful today. But I want to thank both of you for clothing yourselves not only in your wedding clothes, but with compassion, kindness, and love—and for helping all of us understand a little bit better just what Christmas is all about."

As I headed back to my seat, the entire room seemed to rise to their feet, clapping and shouting, "Hallelujah!" Even the pastors joined in, laughing and praising God. But after several moments, Pastor Rodriquez held up both hands for quiet. His eyes twinkled. "It seems the *celebración* has begun! But before I can let you all go downstairs to party, we have one more important thing we must do."

Chairs creaked as everyone sat down.

"Josh and Edesa, I now pronounce you husband and wife—and mom and dad!"

AND THEN WE *did* party! During the service, Ricardo Enriquez's *mariachi* band had sneaked in through the alley door and were still setting up their instruments and sound system. Tables along both sides of the room groaned with food—the inevitable macaroni and cheese, sliced ham and hot rolls, fruit salads, several versions of rice and beans, enchiladas, platters of veggies and dips, and cute little pastries filled with spinach and cream cheese. Several Manna House teens manned the punch bowl—a tangy red punch with lime sherbet floating in it, which was going over big with the younger set.

Instead of a receiving line, Josh and Edesa just mingled with their guests in the downstairs dining room, greeting people, introducing Gracie, smiling until I'm sure their mouths hurt. A crowd gathered around the Sisulu-Smiths, peppering them with questions about their recent time in South Africa. I wanted to eavesdrop, but felt obligated to introduce Denny's and my parents to the pastors and others who greeted them.

"Yo! Jodi!" Yo-Yo, her hands full with a plate of food and a plastic glass of punch, elbowed me in the side. "Didn't know you could preach like that!"

I opened my mouth to rebut her teasing . . . and instead said, "Whoa. You look great!" For the first time since I'd known her, Yo-Yo was *not* wearing a pair of overalls or cargo pants with big pockets. Instead, she wore black slacks, low sling-back heels, and a soft, silvery, jersey top with a scoop neck and little cap sleeves. A single-strand, silver cross necklace complemented the scoop neck, along with simple silver earrings. A fresh cut, color, and lots of gel gave her the cute, pixie hairstyle that seemed to be her trademark.

She gave me a lopsided grin. "Like it? Ruth took me to the Gap. What can I say?"

Ben Garfield was busy snapping pictures with his new digital camera, and at one point rounded up all the Yada Yadas for a group portrait. "The bride in the middle," he bossed. "No, no, I can't see Yo-Yo. Come to the front, *gelibte* . . ."

"Huh. Can't never tell if he's saying somethin' nice or cussin' me out," Yo-Yo complained, reluctantly moving to the front of our little crowd.

"It means sweetheart," Ruth hissed. "Now smile, or I'll call you something not so nice." At that we all laughed and Ben snapped his picture.

As people finished eating, Josh took off his jacket, stood on a chair, and hung a brightly colored *piñata* in the shape of a donkey. "Yeaaa!" the kids yelled. Out came a plastic bat and a blindfold, and Josh—ever the kid himself—lined up the kids along one wall according to height. Most of the adults bunched nervously along the other walls, afraid the swinging bat might come flying. Littlest kids got three tries, bigger kids got two—and finally Michael Sisulu-Smith whacked open the *piñata*, setting up a squealing melee as the kids scrambled for the rain of candy.

"And now . . ." Ricardo Enriquez clapped for attention, a wide smile on his rugged face. " . . . we dance! First, the happy couple." He turned to his band. "One, two, three—"

Josh, in his rolled-up shirtsleeves and red vest, led Edesa—minus the long *mantilla*—into the middle of the room, and they began to dance. The song sounded familiar, and then I remembered. It was the same song Ricardo had played at the La Fiesta Restaurant when Josh and Edesa had announced their engagement. My eyes teared up as I watched my son and his new bride, not slow dancing, but whirling each other around, laughing. I closed my eyes, capturing the moment in my mind's eye. *Oh Jesus! Whatever life holds for them, don't let them lose their joy . . .*

I was so busy silently praying that Josh surprised me when he grabbed my hand with a teasing grin. "May I have this dance, *Mamacita*?" Edesa had already snagged Denny, but it didn't last long as Peter Douglass, Carl Hickman, Mark Smith, and even Denny's dad kept cutting in on the bride. It was easy for me to dance with Josh—he was a good dancer, easily taking the lead, making me feel as if I could dance, too, in spite of the elastic bandage still wrapped around my ankle and the rod in my left thigh.

And then the room was full of dancers, even the kids, as the happy music of mariachi violins, guitars, and drums filled the dining room of the Manna House shelter. No one needed a partner—though Chanda's thirteen-year-old son, Tom, looking manly in his dress shirt and tie, managed to finagle a dance with twelve-year-old Carla Hickman, who didn't seem to mind at all.

I found refuge in a chair after my dance with Josh, and then watched José and Amanda dancing together, both of them rebuffing any efforts on the part of others to cut in. Florida guessed my thoughts as she flopped down in the chair beside me, mopping sweat from her face. "Mm-hm. I'm thinkin' them two just parked that 'just friends' nonsense and got their little romance back in gear."

Well. So be it, Lord. They're in Your hands now. But I smiled. *After Mr. Tallahassee, José Enriquez is a gem. A real gem.*

It was almost as fun watching the dancers as dancing ourselves. Chanda—who, true to her word, came "decked out" in four-inch silver heels and a silvery dress that hugged her hips and fell in flounces at her knees—seemed determined to dance with every man in the room. Silver-haired Ben Garfield schlepped past us with Ruth in his arms, who was panting, "*Oy!* So fast you have to go?" while Chris and Cedric Hickman gallantly cavorted with two-year-old Havah and Isaac Garfield, making everyone laugh.

No one noticed that Josh and Edesa were missing until they reappeared in street clothes carrying Gracie and a bulging diaper bag. They cut Denny and me out of the herd like a good cow pony might. "Here she is, Mom." Josh handed the baby to me and the diaper bag to his dad. The frilly baby dress had been replaced by a soft flannel sleeper and a warm blanket. "Dad, the porta-crib is in your car. Thanks so much for being willing to keep her this week-end . . . and thank the grandparents for the use of their car tonight."

Edesa leaned in to kiss the baby, and then kissed me on the cheek. "*Gracias,* Jodi. I just fed and changed her; she should be all right for a while. Feed her again when you get home, and she should sleep till about three or four in the morning." With assur-ances that the bag contained bottles, formula, lots of disposable diapers, a pacifier, several changes of clothes, and written instruc-tions, the pair headed up the stairs, followed by a herd of chatter-ing guests who wanted to see them off and shower them with wild birdseed—the city-friendly version of throwing rice.

But I stayed behind, Gracie in my lap. The weight of her in my arms, the softness of her one-piece sleeper, and the powdery smell of her latte skin made her seem so . . . *real.* I touched the soft dark hair trying to curl on top, then traced her ear and cheek with my finger. At my touch, Gracie's dark eyes focused on mine, and she reached with one hand toward my face. I caught two of her fingers in my mouth. Her face dimpled into an open-mouthed grin, like a silent baby laugh.

I could hardly breathe.

If all went as hoped with the adoption, this little girl, Gracie Francesca, was my granddaughter.

Me. A grandmother.

18

A *baby was crying . . . somewhere . . . why didn't its mother pick it up? . . . still crying . . . there, it stopped . . . that's better . . . oh no, crying again . . . better find the mother . . . why can't I find the mother? . . . what if, oh no, what if she abandoned the baby? . . . better get help—*

I sat up with a start. The room was dark. But the crying was—

Gracie! I threw back the bedcovers. Oh no! How long had she been crying? The glowing numbers on the alarm clock said *4:10*. Stuffing my feet into a pair of slippers, I hustled to the porta-crib at the end of our bed. "Shh, shh." I picked up the squalling infant and a blanket, fishing in the dark for her pacifier. What lungs! The whole house was probably awake by now.

Tiptoeing to the door with the baby tucked in my arms, I glanced back at the bed, where presumably that large lump under the covers was my husband. The lump didn't move. *Humph.* Seemed like I remembered this same scenario when our kids were little.

"Hold on, sweetie, hold on," I murmured, scurrying toward the kitchen in the darkened house, lit only by a night-light in the hallway. Juggling Gracie, still wailing, in one arm, I pulled a bottle of formula from the refrigerator, put it in a pan in the sink, and ran hot water over it as I jiggled and paced and shushed.

When the warm milk passed the drop-on-the-inside-of-the-wrist test, I cradled Gracie in the crook of my arm, poked the nipple into her hungry mouth, and watched in satisfaction as she latched on and began to suck. Slowly I carried her into the living room, where I awkwardly bent down with my bundle to plug in the Christmas tree lights. *Ahh, magic.* The reflection of multicolored lights danced in the dark windows and on the ceiling and walls. I started to settle into the recliner, when I remembered.

It's Christmas morning! I had another Babe to take care of.

Amanda had already moved the Mary and Joseph figures into the stable under the tree last night after the wedding. Now, searching for the little wooden "Baby Jesus," I finally found it on a window ledge and put it into the tiny manger inside the stable. Spying the shepherd figures and their sheep on the coffee table, I moved them under the tree as well. After all, the shepherds had "made haste" after they got the glorious news from the choir of angels in the middle of the night.

With Baby Jesus tucked into the manger, I finally settled down in the recliner with Gracie, her cuddle blanket, and an extra afghan. She'd already drunk half the bottle, but her eyes were wide open. Good thing I didn't have school on Monday! But once I quit moving around, Gracie's eyelids fluttered and sagged . . . and by the time the bottle neared empty, her eyes had closed. The nipple slid out of her mouth. Her breathing steadied.

Should I put her back in the porta-crib? Probably. But I didn't move. I didn't want this moment to end. Josh and Edesa's soon-to-be adopted child—my granddaughter—asleep in my arms . . . the hush of early Christmas morning, as if the world was standing on the cusp of a glorious sunrise . . .

THE SMELL OF yeast and cinnamon tickled my nose. Gracie stirred on my lap. My arms ached. I opened my eyes to see the windows framing the pale blue light of morning. I looked down; Gracie's round eyes were staring up at me.

I grinned. "Merry Christmas, little one." I carefully slid out of the chair, shifting the baby to my shoulder, and followed my nose into the kitchen. My mother, wearing pink fuzzy slippers and an apron over a faded pink robe, was taking a large pan of bubbling cinnamon rolls out of the oven. Coffee gurgled and dripped from the coffeemaker.

"Mom! When did you have time to make cinnamon rolls? I mean, don't they have to rise and all that? *Uhh*. Take Gracie a minute, will you? I've got to stretch my muscles."

My mother, her cheeks flushed, her gray hair askew, took Gracie from me. "Pooh. Too many questions. Put some cups on that tray, will you? Uh-oh. You need changing, little girl. Where's her diaper bag?"

By the time my dad, Denny, and Amanda wandered sleepy-eyed into the living room, Gracie had dry pants, had inhaled a morning bottle, and was kicking her legs on a blanket in front of the tree, fascinated by the lights and dangling ornaments. I'd popped the turkey into the oven for a two o'clock dinner, sneaking it into one of those newfangled "roasting bags," because who had time to baste that sucker! A Christmas CD filled the air with carols. And the tray of tempting cinnamon rolls, coffee, and orange juice sat ready on the coffee table.

"Mm," said Amanda, her mouth full of buttery cinnamon roll. "What time is church? Can we open our stockings now?"

The quilted Christmas stockings I'd made years ago for Denny and the kids and me hung fat and bulging from tiny nails along the middle window frames of our bay windows, along with cheap red fuzzy stockings we'd picked up last week at the Dollar Store for the grandparents and Edesa. *THAT'S what I should have made for Josh and Edesa's wedding gift,* I thought. *Christmas stockings! Maybe I could still—*

The back doorbell bleated, along with several loud raps on the door window. Denny leaped to his feet and headed for the kitchen. "I'll get it."

I heard murmuring and whispering. What was going on? But half a minute later Stu and Estelle stuck their heads around the living room archway. "Merry Christmas, everybody! No, don't get up . . . we're off to Indianapolis to have Christmas dinner with my parents," Stu said. "Pray that we make it okay—weather report says rain mixed with snow. *Ugh.* Pray for Avis and Peter too. They're on their way to Ohio. Bye, Mr. and Mrs. Jennings—you'll probably be gone by the time we get back on Tuesday." They waved and were gone.

Tuesday. Stu was on the Yada Yada reunion committee. I hadn't heard any plans yet. Sure hoped that left enough time to get it together before New Year's Day.

Amanda reluctantly agreed to "do stockings" after church when the rest of the family arrived for dinner. SouledOut had announced a short worship service at eleven o'clock for this Sunday since it was also Christmas Day, giving families time to do their Christmas morning festivities. I half-wished we could skip church today and just hang out at home . . . until we walked into the storefront sanctuary with five minutes to spare and saw the Sisulu-Smith family surrounded by excited SouledOut members. Some of the younger kids, who couldn't quite remember who these people were, nonetheless seemed fascinated by Nonyameko's curious accent and the boys' dashikis. Every female in the place had her eyes on Nony's beautiful black-and-gold tunic and head wrap she'd worn yesterday to the wedding.

I caught Nony's eye, and she managed to slip away from the clutch of well-wishers. "Good morning, Sister Jodi." She smiled the same radiant smile I remembered so well. "So. *Ugogo*—grandmother—has the baby today."

"No, my mom can't—" I felt my face flush. "Oh. You mean *me*."

Nony laughed. "Yes, you, Jodi. Wasn't Joshua a junior in high school when we first met? And now he has married our Edesa and handed you a Latina grandchild! So much has happened since we went away."

"Oh, Nony," I said, wiping my eyes. "I've missed you so much. Now here you are, and I haven't had even two minutes with you to myself."

"I have missed you, too, Jodi. You are not teaching this week, correct? We will be packing up our house, but I will slip away one day and we can have lunch, yes?"

She scribbled her new cell phone number on a scrap of paper just as the praise team launched into *Joy to the world! The Lord is come!*" The island beat of their rendition had everyone standing, clapping, and praising to the joyous Christmas carol. "Yes, yes, yes," I whispered, giving Nony a hug with my free arm. Then, baby carrier in tow, I scurried to the seat Denny had saved for me.

BY THE TIME we got home, the succulent smell of roast turkey filled the house. I put everyone to work on dinner and table setting. Denny's parents showed up at one o'clock in a taxi, having declined our invitation to come to worship at SouledOut that morning in favor of a leisurely morning at their hotel. Fifteen minutes later, Josh and Edesa, flushed and grinning ear to ear, pulled up in my parents' aging sedan. All that was missing from the general hubbub as everyone hugged and wished each other "Merry Christmas!" was Willie Wonka's excited barking.

I felt a pang. The old dog had been gone two Christmases now. *Wonka would have loved Gracie,* I thought. He'd always been so protective with Amanda when she was little.

Even though we'd had many hands and laps to take care of Gracie the last eighteen hours, I was relieved when she was back in Edesa's arms. Caring for a grandbaby was going to take some getting used to.

At two o'clock, we gathered around the table as an extended family for the first time and lit the white Christmas candle in the middle of our Advent wreath. Denny asked my father to bless the food—a mistake, I thought, since my dad tended to pray not only for every single person at the table, but all the missing family members by name and a list of missionaries too. But finally, the platter of sliced turkey and bowls of bread stuffing, mashed potatoes, gravy, green beans, and fruit salad made the rounds, along with the requisite cranberry sauce, pickles and olives, and hot bakery rolls, amid much teasing and laughter.

"The Watch Night service your Pastor Cobbs announced this morning sounds interesting," my father said during a lull. "I didn't realize New Year's Eve had special significance for blacks in this country."

"Oh?" Harley Baxter heaped seconds of everything on his plate. "New Year's Eve is *party* time in New York, right, Kay?" He winked at his wife.

"Mm. Watch Night service . . . how quaint," Kay Harley murmured sweetly.

"Yeah, the youth group's been doing most of the planning," Amanda chimed in. "We're supposed to invite neighborhood teens."

Josh turned to Edesa. "I wonder . . . do you think we could bring the kids from Manna House that night?"

Sheesh! I wanted to shake him. *You just got married! You have a baby already! One thing at a time, kiddo!* But I kept my mouth shut and cleared the table. Somewhere in the back of my mind, I remembered something Nony had said at the time Josh graduated from high school . . .

"God has plans for that young man, Jodi. Not your plans. Don't stand in his way. I believe God will use your Joshua like the Joshua of old, to fight a battle that the older generation will not fight."

"Pie in the living room!" I announced. But in my heart I said, *Okay, Lord. Thanks for reminding me that Josh is Yours, no longer mine.*

Opening the stocking gifts was fun. "Who snuck these breath mints in here? Somebody trying to tell me something?" . . . "Sardines! Awriiiight." . . . "Dad! This ankle bracelet has to be from you." . . . "A pacifier—no, three pacifiers! Hey, how come these ended up in my stocking instead of Edesa's?"

Both Josh and Edesa seemed delighted by the Christmas ornaments Denny and I had sneaked into their stockings—a "Just Married" bride and groom in Josh's, and a "Baby's First Christmas" in Edesa's.

By the time the stockings were empty, we each had a pile of goodies, both useful and silly, in our laps. I was somewhat bemused by the furry toy mouse I found in my stocking, but no one owned up to it.

Kay and Harley were the first to leave, saying they had a plane to catch at six. We talked my parents into staying over until the next day, in order to drive home by daylight. "Besides, Grandpa, we need your car one more night," Josh teased. "Chanda George gave us *two* nights at the Orrington, remember? Mom, you and Dad okay with Gracie one more night?"

"Oh, sure," I said, taking Gracie once more. "Maybe you can't teach an old dog new tricks, but I seem to remember a few old ones. We'll be fine."

I stood at the bay window and watched them pull away in my parents' car. Then I bent down and kissed the baby's forehead, breathing in the sweet smell of her skin. "But I'm kicking your grandpa out of bed for the two o'clock feeding, kiddo," I murmured.

BY THE TIME I got Gracie fed, changed, burped, rocked, and finally down in the porta-crib, Denny and my parents had all the dirty dishes in the dishwasher and leftovers put away. Amanda disappeared into her room with the phone—to José, no doubt—and my parents said they were tired and wanted to retire early.

"Are we alone?" Denny asked. I was curled up on the couch with a mug of hot peppermint tea, enjoying a "Christmas Around the World" CD.

"Mm." I patted the couch cushions beside me. "Come sit, enjoy the tree."

"Uh, be there in just a minute." He disappeared.

A few moments later, I heard footsteps above my head in Stu's apartment. *What in the world?* I knew Stu and Estelle weren't home yet . . . what was Denny doing up there?

The back door banged shut, then Denny poked his head into the living room. "Close your eyes."

"What?"

"Close your eyes!"

I closed them. What was he up to?

"Okay. You can look."

I opened my eyes. A cardboard box shaped like a house sat under the Christmas tree. A box with holes in it. Soft scratching and a mewing sound came from inside.

"Denny! What—?" I was at the tree in three steps. I opened the box and peered inside. Two small kittens peered up at me. "Oh, Denny," I breathed.

I reached inside and lifted out both kittens, one in each hand. One was mostly black with white paws, a white muzzle, with a black splotch on its nose. The other was a calico—orange and black and white splotches from head to tail.

"Oh, Denny," I said again, burying my face into their soft fur. The black-and-white one licked my chin.

"Merry Christmas, babe," Denny said softly.

175

19

*J*osh and Edesa arrived early the next morning to pick up Gracie so my parents could get on the road. While Denny was delivering them to the Hickman Hilton, as we dubbed their tiny apartment, along with the porta-crib, a stash of wedding presents, and turkey leftovers, I called Ruth to wish her Happy Hanukkah.

The eight-day Jewish Festival of Lights began the day after Christmas that year. But of course I couldn't resist telling her about Denny's surprise—especially when both of them were tumbling around my feet, playing with the shoelaces on my gym shoes.

"He what? Gave you a kitten? What kind of *mishigas* is that?"

I giggled. "*Two* kittens. He figured two would keep each other company when we have to be away at work. He conspired with Stu, who had them penned up in her bathroom for two days. But you should see them, Ruth. They're adorable."

"Adorable, schmorable. Twice the trouble, Jodi. *Oy vey.* I should know. Some potato latkes you should make for Hanukkah. Or honey puffs. A good recipe I have—Isaac! No! Put that box down! . . ." Ruth's voice faded into the distance, accompanied by much squealing. Then I heard a screech. "Havah, stop! Stop! . . . Ben, catch her! . . . *Oy gevalt!* Not on the rug!" The phone went dead.

I grinned at the phone. Potato latkes sounded good. I'd ask for the recipe when I called back later. Much later.

Amanda came into the kitchen and swooped up the calico kitten. "Mom! You *have* to call this one Patches. How about Peanut for the black one? Patches and Peanut, that's cute. But do you *have* to keep the litter box in the bathroom? Gross."

"Hm. Maybe we'll keep it in your bedroom, 'Manda. After all, you're not there much . . ."

She rolled her eyes and muttered, "Better not."

I knew now why Denny had waited until Christmas night to give me his surprise. Patches and Peanut (well, why not?) were, well, three-month-old *kittens*, getting into *everything*. No dust bunny, pant leg, scrap of paper, or bare toe was off-limits as far as they were concerned. *It moves! Pounce on it!*

In spite of their antics, the week after Christmas felt like a long soak in a Japanese spa after the mad scrabble events of last week— not to mention the surprise arrival of the Sisulu-Smiths. Which reminded me . . .

I called Nony's cell phone to see when we could get together for lunch, and we settled on Thursday at the Heartland Café. "I hear we are planning a Yada Yada reunion, a 'big splash,' to use Chanda's words." Nony seemed hesitant. "I do not want to spoil any plans, but . . . to tell you the truth, my sister, I would treasure getting together with just my Yada Yada sisters to share, to pray, to worship as we did for two years before I went home to South Africa."

My mind scrambled. I hadn't heard yet from the "reunion committee" about the plans for Sunday, but Chanda had pushed for a big party with kids and spouses, party clothes, music and dancing—

Which is exactly what we did at the wedding reception! When planning the reunion, we hadn't expected Nony's family to arrive in time for the wedding. But now . . .

"Sounds good to me, Nony. I'll pass that along. See you Thursday!"

Yikes. Who was on the committee? Adele, Chanda, Avis, Stu . . . Stu. I'd heard footsteps walking around upstairs earlier. She and Estelle must be home by now. I'd tell Stu and let her handle it.

I ducked out the back door without a jacket and up the outdoor steps to the second floor apartment. Estelle must have heard me coming because she opened the door before I even knocked. "Get in here, girl. Where's your coat? My bones are creaking bad enough without seeing you freezing out there. Sit down. I was just making some hot tea. How are you makin' out with them baby cats?"

"That's right. You guys were in on the surprise. I love 'em! They are so cute."

"Good. Because they are *not* coming back up here. Now go on, sit."

I sat. *Sheesh.* It felt so good just to sit and drink tea with Stu and Estelle, no papers to grade, no wedding to plan, no holiday dinner to cook. We chatted for half an hour before I remembered what I had come up for. I told them what Nony had said about the reunion, and saw Stu and Estelle exchange looks.

"What?"

Stu grinned. "Great minds think alike. Estelle and I had the same thought coming home from Indianapolis—that we already had our blowout party at the wedding reception! Nothing against the hubbies and kids, but . . . what we need now is time to get down with our sisters." Stu sat back and grinned. "At least we can blame the change on a request from Nony."

STU MUST HAVE got on the phone with the rest of the committee because, sure enough, an e-mail was sitting in my in-box the next time I booted up the computer.

To: Yada Yada
From: YY Reunion Committee
           GetRealStu@GetReal.com
Re: YY Reunion—natch!

Listen up, sisters! WHEREAS it would be hard to compete with the REVELRY we all enjoyed at the Baxter-Reyes wedding, which was A. family friendly; B. a chance to gussy up in our finest; C. alive with music and dancing; and D. attended by all Yada Yadas, spouses, and kidlets were . . .

And WHEREAS one of our Guests of Honor has specifically requested a reunion with "just us Yada Yadas" . . .

Just then Peanut took a leap, landed on the desk, and walked across the computer keys. "Hey, you!" I plucked the black-and-white kitten off the keyboard, nuzzled his cute little wet nose, and snuggled him in my lap as I read on.

. . . The Reunion Committee is hereby recommending we schedule our reunion to coincide with our first Yada Yada meeting of the New Year, this Sunday, same time, at Jodi Baxter's domicile (she's next on the list to host). Never fear, we WILL party the Yada Yada Way—Play and Pray. So bring your favorite Christmas goody, your favorite worship CD, and a simple MEMORY GIFT for your SECRET SISTER, whose name will be drawn by a non-Yada Yada third party and sent to each of you by separate e-mail.

The Reunion Committee
Avis, Stu, Adele, and Chanda

Oh, right. Avis did *not* write that e-mail. Stu just put her name first to lend weight to the "recommendation."

I checked e-mail again just before heading down the street late Thursday morning to meet Nony for lunch. Ah, there it was, an e-mail with "Secret Sister" in the subject line, though I had no idea who Rock-a-BabyJ@online.net was—oh, wait. That sounded like Rochelle Johnson, Avis's daughter. The message simply said: "Jodi Baxter, your Secret Sister is Adele Skuggs."

Adele . . . whoa. That would take some serious thinking what to do for her.

But I shoved it to the back of my mind, bundled up against the damp, just-above-freezing weather, and walked the few blocks to the Heartland Café. After weeks on my crutches, it felt good to walk.

Nony was already seated at a table in the funky café, sipping a cup of coffee. Today she was dressed in jeans and a sweatshirt with a UKZN logo. "Do they need *sweatshirts* in KwaZulu-Natal?" I teased.

Nony's eyes laughed at me over the rim of her coffee cup. "No. But I need it *here.*"

A waiter in jeans and a Heartland Café T-shirt brought us menus. Nony ordered the "Three-Scoop Salad Plate" with hummus, guacamole, and tuna salad with pita bread. "Make it two," I said. Truth to tell, I felt too lazy to make a decision.

I could have listened to Nony's South African lilt all day, but she wanted to know all the news in our family for the past year and a half. "Nony! You *know* all about Josh and Edesa. Amanda is in her first year at the University of Illinois, living in a dorm. So far it's been 'no news is good news.' Haven't seen her grades. Denny's still athletic director at West Rogers High, and me, I'm still riding herd on third graders at Bethune Elementary. That's it! Oh, except . . . remember Hakim? He's the brother, uh . . . " I let it hang. It was still hard to say the words, *"the brother of the boy I killed."*

Nony placed her hand on mine. "I remember, though I never met him."

I told her what had happened earlier that month, the purse snatching, the fall, discovering Hakim's role in it all. "He's not a bad kid, Nony. I can tell he's trying to make it up to me—maybe he even wants me to know. But . . . I don't think his mother wants us to connect again. Too many painful memories."

Nony could barely hide her smile. "Maybe so. But God is at work, Jodi! Yes, I know it. Do not worry about what happens next. God will show you."

Our food arrived. Nony held my hand and prayed aloud, earning strange looks from other tables. I didn't care . . . well, maybe a little. God would have heard us if we'd *whispered* a prayer of thanks, wouldn't He?

"Now you," I insisted, tearing my pita bread and dipping it in the hummus. "Tell me about the boys. How is Mark doing?"

"Marcus and Michael . . . no longer my *boykies*, as you can see. Doing well in school. Enjoying their small celebrity status as *American* blacks." Mark's memory and coordination continued to improve, she said, though the loss of vision in the one eye often left him frustrated. "But we praise our God it is only his eye, and not his life, that was lost." She sank into her own thoughts and memories for a moment.

"And you, Nony?"

She shook her head. "Oh, Jodi. The situation in my country is far worse than I realized. Or maybe I knew it in my head, but to see it every day . . . " The picture she painted of the AIDS pandemic wasn't pretty. The province of KwaZulu-Natal had the highest rate of HIV infection in all of South Africa. Thousands, even millions, of children orphaned. "I have been working with a Christian teacher in one of the schools, teaching HIV/AIDS education, as well as Bible values about respecting our bodies, respecting others, waiting until marriage, being faithful to one's spouse . . . but sometimes I feel so overwhelmed, Jodi. There is still so much ignorance! What I am doing is like trying to empty the ocean with a spoon."

I didn't know what to say. At least she was doing *something*.

My plate of food was almost gone. Nony picked at hers. "But we cannot lose hope. Mark is helping to create some symposiums at the university, bringing together political, religious, and educational leaders to show that this problem must be dealt with on all levels, working together. That is one reason we have decided to stay—you know how Mark is when he gets a tiger by the tail." She smiled slightly.

Oh boy, did I. Professor Mark Smith had waded head-on into the fray when a white-supremacist group had dared to recruit on Northwestern University's campus—a tiger-by-the-tail that had left him in a coma for weeks. We Yada Yadas had learned just how real spiritual warfare was—and it toughened our prayer knees. The perpetrators were now sitting in prison serving a long sentence for attempted murder, and the racist group had fractured. Score a big one for God.

Suddenly Nony leaned forward, her dark eyes intense under her sculptured braids. "But I have this idea that won't leave me alone. I want you to pray with me, Jodi. Many young women in the townships, destitute and desperate, turn to sex just to survive—but they pay for it with their beautiful lives. I want to help women start their own businesses—weaving rugs and dyeing cloth, selling them, earning their own income to give them pride, to give them a choice to stay pure and safe . . . "

I smiled inwardly. This was the Nony I knew. Passionate. Determined. On fire. We talked until the waiter removed our plates and brought the check. She suddenly jumped up. "Oh, I must go. By the way, if there is anything you want from our house, Jodi, just come and get it. We have to sell most everything except our personal items."

We walked out of the funky neighborhood café together. "Pray with me, Jodi. I will ask Yada Yada too. If I know anything, I know this: unless the Lord builds the house, we labor in vain. If this idea is of God, I need prayer warriors."

"Absolutely." We hugged, and I watched as she unlocked her car and pulled out of her parking space, pausing as she drove under the el overpass for a small group of boys sauntering across the street. I squinted. One of the boys looked familiar. Could it—

"Hakim!" I waved, my heart pounding. "Hakim! Come here a sec, okay?"

The boys paused, their shoulders hunched, glancing uneasily in my direction. But Hakim separated himself from the other two boys and ambled in my direction. "Hey, Miz B. How ya doin'?"

"Hey, yourself." I smiled to put him at ease. "I missed you when you shoveled our walk last time. Say, how about some hot chocolate?" I jerked my thumb at the café. "Your friends, too, if you'd like." *Please Lord, just Hakim, not the friends . . .*

"Ah, I dunno, Miz B." Hakim glanced back at his companions. "They don't want to. Maybe another time."

"Please, Hakim. They've got great Mexican hot chocolate here. I'm paying." I smiled and lifted an inviting eyebrow, knowing I was pitting White Woman versus Homeboys. Stupid me. But I held my ground.

Finally he shrugged. "Guess so." He waved his buddies away . . . and five minutes later we were back at the same table Nony and I had just vacated, this time with huge, soup-bowl-size mugs of Mexican hot chocolate with whipped cream and chocolate shavings on top. Just looking at it put pounds on my hips.

"So . . . I was glad to see you and your mom at Manna House last Saturday."

He shrugged. "She made me come. It was all right, I guess. But Mom and me—we don't get along too good. Mostly I stay with my aunt and my cousins."

"Why is that, Hakim?"

Another shrug. "She's so . . . so strict, Miz B. Won't let me do nuthin'! Won't let me hang with my friends, wants me home right after school. She grounds me all the time. I got fed up, ran away a few times. Finally, she agreed to let me stay at my aunt's. It's okay, I guess." He busied himself with his hot chocolate.

Tread lightly, Jodi. "She's scared, Hakim."

His head jerked up, whipped cream across his upper lip. "Whatchu mean?"

"She's scared she'll lose you too—like your brother, Jamal." There. It was out on the table, the tragedy that bound us together forever.

He frowned. "What happened to Jamal don't have nothin' to do with me. And I don't blame you for it, Miz B. You know that."

"I know, Hakim," I said softly. "That means a lot to me." I paused, praying in my spirit without words. After a long moment I said, "Hakim, I know that you and your friends are the ones who snatched my purse that night. I wanted to tell you."

To my surprise, he didn't jump and run. Didn't deny it. Didn't do anything. Just sat there, gripping that big ol' mug. But after a few moments, his tortured eyes met mine. "You gonna tell the police?" he whispered.

I shook my head.

"Why?"

"Because I forgive you, Hakim. And I think you've been trying to make it right."

With a jerk, he brushed the back of his hand across his eyes. I busied myself with my calorie-loaded hot chocolate, knowing he didn't want me to see him cry. Finally he mumbled, "I'm real sorry, Miz B. Sorry you got hurt. It wasn't s'posed to be like that."

"I know." I leaned forward. "But I do have a favor to ask. It would mean a lot."

He frowned. "What?"

"New Year's Eve . . . our church is having a Watch Night service—

at SouledOut Community Church, up there in the Howard Street Mall. It's especially for youth. Nine o'clock. Will you come?"

He looked surprised. "That your church? I seen that up there in the mall." He shrugged. "Guess so. If my stupid mom will let me stay out till midnight—"

"Bring your mom too."

He snorted and rolled his eyes. "Yeah, *right*."

I let that one go, paid our bill, and we walked out onto the sidewalk together. "Thanks, Hakim. I'm glad we got that squared away. But, um, I've got a question. My husband said you had a black eye and some cuts on your face when you came to the house last time. What happened?"

A lopsided smile eased the tension on his face. "Oh, that. Had to fight my cousin to get them credit cards of yours back. Sorry about the cash, though."

"Oh! Well, thanks. I appreciate it." I didn't have the heart to tell him the cards were worthless. He'd gotten that black eye for nothing . . . No, I was wrong. He'd fought for his self-respect and to make things right.

20

$\mathcal{J}$ had no idea if Hakim would take me up on my invitation, but I felt like dancing anyway. Nobody but God could have timed that "accidental" meeting outside the Heartland Café. Now Hakim knew I knew about the purse snatching. He knew I forgave him. He knew I still cared about him and wanted to be friends. All the doors had been left open.

Had to watch that Mexican hot chocolate, though.

With New Year's weekend coming up and a whole week of school vacation after that, I felt giddy enough Friday morning to call Edesa and ask if she and Josh would like to come for supper Saturday before the Watch Night service. "It's the sixth day of Hanukkah," I said. "I want to try out Ruth's recipe for potato latkes. Want to come?"

"*Sí!* We would love to, Jodi. Except . . . would tonight be all right instead? We will be at Manna House Saturday afternoon and are bringing a vanload of kids to the Watch Night service."

"Oh, right. I forgot. Tonight, then. Just be sure to bring Gracie with you!" *And take her home again.* Hadn't I heard that somewhere? Oh yeah, a little magnet on my mom's refrigerator. *"A perfect grandparent loves them, spoils them—then sends them home."* Sounded good to me!

I called Ruth to get her recipe for latkes. "Um, what happened the other day when I called? Sounded like the twins had a meltdown."

Ruth snorted in my ear. *"Oy vey!* The little *nudniks.* Isaac dumped a box of matzo meal I'd just opened—table, floor, everywhere! Then Havah danced in it and ran into the living room. *Oy yoy yoy.* An hour it took me to clean up matzo, floor, rug, kids! A word of wisdom, Jodi. Don't let those kittens get in your matzo meal."

I laughed, remembering the canister of flour I'd dumped in my haste last week. "Ha. I'm perfectly capable of making my own mess. Now, about the latkes . . . "

The recipe sounded simple enough. Grated potatoes, chopped onions, a little matzo meal, salt, pepper, baking powder . . . shaped into pancakes and then fried. "Serve them with applesauce and sour cream," she said.

"Mm. I don't have sour cream. What about cottage cheese?"

"Cottage cheese?! Only a *goyim* would do that!"

"Um, so I guess bacon or sausage on the side would be out . . . "

I heard a big sigh. "If you *must*, there is such a thing as kosher sausage."

Oh, well, I thought as we hung up. I had to shop for groceries sometime this weekend anyway. Might as well be today.

As I pulled the car into the parking lot at the Howard Street shopping center, I noticed the lights were on in the SouledOut storefront. Even though the church was at the far end from the huge Dominick's grocery that anchored the mall, I parked near the church and stuck my head in the door. Rose Cobbs and a few other women were packing up the Christmas tree decorations. A couple of teenagers stood on ladders taking down the Christmas banner and hanging a new one—made by Estelle, I guessed, because she stood at the back like a traffic cop. "Move the right side up another inch, can you? . . . No, no, too high . . . That's good, that's good."

"Hi, everybody!" I chirped. "I'm on my way to Dominick's. Anybody want me to pick up some coffee or something at the café?" *Duh.* The words were no sooner out of my mouth than I remembered telling First Lady Rose that I'd like to have coffee with her "soon." How many weeks ago was that?

The pastor's wife smiled. "Thank you, Sister Jodi, we're fine. We've got the coffeepot on. But we were going to stop in a few minutes to pray for the Watch Night service tomorrow night. Would you like to join us?"

I hesitated. I needed to get my shopping done and get back home to make supper. I had company coming . . . but the Holy Spirit nudged me. *Pray, Jodi. Lives are at stake. You invited Hakim, remember? There's a battle going on. Pray.*

I WAS GLAD I'd stopped to pray. For one thing, it helped remind me that my Yada Yada sisters weren't the only "praying sisters" I had in the body of believers. I was touched by the fervent prayers of Rose Cobbs, Estelle, and the two other SouledOut sisters praying for our own youth, praying for the neighborhood youth who had been invited, praying for families and friends of our members that were in town, praying that God would "send us out" in the new year.

That, plus I made a date with First Lady Rose to have coffee next week before school started. A good way to start the new year.

The potato latkes were a big hit with my family, hot out of the frying pan, crisp and golden, with lots of chunky applesauce, sour cream, and kosher sausage. We even came up with a makeshift menorah: eight votive candles in a row in the center of the table, plus a tall one for the *shamash*, the center candle used to light the others. As we passed the *shamash* and lit five of the candles, we recited the blessing Ruth and Ben had taught us: "Blessed are You, Lord our God, King of the universe, Who performed wondrous deeds for our ancestors, in those days, at this season."

"That's beautiful." Josh seemed especially thoughtful after we lit the menorah candles. "I really like the way Jewish festivals help them remember God's faithfulness. It seems a great way to pass on 'the faith of our fathers' to the children." He looked at Gracie, tucked in the crook of Denny's arm, chuckling as her new grandpa made faces at her. "I hope Edesa and I can build these kinds of spiritual traditions into our family."

I listened in awe as Josh talked about *"our family."* For a moment, I felt like an historical relic. Whatever we'd done as a family to raise our children was finished. Over. Done. The torch had been passed. Now it was Josh and Edesa who were building a family, using traditions from both sides of the family. His and hers. And theirs. The proverbial "something old, something new." And maybe "something borrowed," too, like this time of remembering at Hanukkah, or the traditional Seder at Passover.

And then I realized *relic* was the wrong word. Here we sat around our dining room table, six of us instead of four, establishing a *new* family tradition—the extended family dinner. Three generations instead of two.

A bubble of anticipation about my new role as mother-in-law and grandmother tickled my spirit. One day Gracie would have a brother or sister, or two or three. And down the road, hopefully, Amanda might get married and the table would get even larger. For a moment, I envisioned the growing table, wondering who . . .

Well, not *Neil* anyway.

I WOKE THE next morning while it was still dark. Denny was snoring softly. *New Year's Eve . . . last day of the year.* I heard Patches and Peanuts scratching the bathroom door, sealing my decision to get up, let the kittens out, and enjoy the Christmas tree, which would be good for another week anyway.

I fed the kittens, made coffee, and had just settled into the recliner with a steaming mug and my Bible when I saw MaDear's jar of buttons sitting on our ancient coffee table. It was sweet of Adele to give them to me—

Ohmigosh! Adele! I nearly spilled my coffee when I remembered. Adele was my Secret Sister, and I was supposed to give her a "memory gift" at our Yada Yada reunion—which was tomorrow! *Ack!* What could I do on such short notice? I eyed the button jar. Unless . . .

By the time Denny and I headed for the Watch Night service at SouledOut Community Church that evening, I'd spent most of the day making my gift for Adele. When we walked into the church at 8:45, the chairs had been stacked out of the way, leaving a large open space. Amanda had come earlier; wouldn't say why. A band made up entirely of youth—wait; was that José Enriquez on the drums?—was already playing a set of contemporary praise music as people arrived. Both pastors plus First Lady Rose and a handful of SouledOut teens acted as greeters, especially trying to make visitors and first-timers welcome.

The fifteen-passenger Manna House van pulled up at 8:55, packed with kids and volunteers from the shelter, followed by a minivan. I recognized Precious and her daughter, Sabrina, in the bunch . . . but so far, I hadn't seen Hakim.

Promptly at nine o'clock, one of the teens in the band took the mic and, in good gospel style, got us clapping and stepping and singing to Israel and New Breed's "I Am Not Forgotten! He Knows My Name!" Amanda and some of the other young women passed out a dozen or more "praise ribbons"—long, wide ribbons attached to a sixteen-inch wand—until the room pulsed with instruments, voices, dancing feet, and a sea of waving ribbons.

Rick Reilly and Oscar Frost, SouledOut's youth leaders, then dedicated the first hour to hilarious games that included everyone: relays, icebreakers, and even "Pin the Diaper on Baby New Year," which turned out to be the funniest of all.

Denny had just volunteered to try his skills at pinning the diaper on Baby New Year, when I felt a tug on my arm. "Hey, Miz B."

"Hakim! You came!"

He grinned and jerked a thumb over his shoulder. "Yeah. My mom an' my Aunt Gwennie too."

Sure enough. Geraldine Wilkins-Porter and another attractive African-American woman with a strong family resemblance to

Hakim's mother stood uncertainly among the laughing crowd, their coats still on. "Mrs. Porter. Welcome to SouledOut. And I'm so glad to meet Hakim's aunt."

The second woman nodded without smiling, but shook my extended hand. Hakim's mother studied me, her eyes guarded. "So. We meet again, Mrs. Baxter. This is *your* church? *You* invited Hakim? I'm not sure we—"

"Yes, I did. I told him to invite you too. I hope that was all right. It's a bit crazy now but—" As if to prove my point, some of the kids screeched and the crowd laughed as a blindfolded Denny stuck the cardboard diaper on Baby New Year's head. I rolled my eyes. "That's my husband up there making a fool of himself."

Hakim's mother frowned. "I was expecting a Watch Night service, not a party."

"I think this is just a warm-up. Please stay—oh! Pastor Cobbs!" I grabbed Joe Cobbs as he passed. "I'd like for you to meet one of my former students and his family. Hakim Porter, his mother . . ."

Thank You, Lord, I breathed, just as the emcee invited everyone to break for refreshments while a crew set up the chairs. Pastor Cobbs had a way of making new people feel like honored guests, and in a moment, he had both women smiling. Finally, this wasn't just about me.

195

21

Fifteen minutes later, the emcee invited everyone to take seats for the next part. We had more people than chairs, so some SouledOut members stood around the walls. Oscar Frost quieted the room with a slow hymn on his saxophone, while Pastor Cobbs stepped onto the six-inch platform to introduce the next part of the evening.

"It's New Year's Eve, people. For many folks, it's simply a secular holiday, a night to party, to ring out the old and ring in the new. However, many churches, especially in the African-American community, have Watch Night services on this night—but do we know why? Let's go back in time and watch as the SouledOut Players bring it to life . . ."

He slipped away as the back half of the room dimmed. Pastor Clark stepped onto the low platform wearing clogs, white tights, knee breeches, a vest, and puffy shirtsleeves. "My name is Count Zinzindorf," he announced soberly. "I live on an estate in Berthelsdorf, Germany. One night a young man came to my door, seeking my protection for a group of Christians from Moravia who were being persecuted for protesting excesses of the state church. I gave them shelter and encouraged them to establish their community on my land."

Pastor Clark certainly looked the part of an eighteenth-century European count with his tall bearing, pale skin, and gray hair. He strode about the platform, his hands animated. "I tell you, I was impressed by their Christ-centered view of the Christian life. So impressed I counted myself among them. These Moravians lived simply, but were extremely generous in giving away their wealth. And their missionary fervor! I'd never seen such zeal to take the good news to those usually ignored—to slaves in various parts of the world and Native Americans in the New World. I threw in my lot with these Moravian brothers, though it meant much opposition and ridicule."

The "Count" paused in mid-stride. "It was these Moravians who first coined the term 'Watch Night' in 1733 to thank God for His blessing and protection in the past year, and to dedicate themselves to God's service in the coming year." Pastor Clark stepped off the stage, hands clasped behind his back, murmuring, "Yes, yes. I was very impressed."

Pastor Cobbs reappeared and picked up the thread. "The Methodists adopted the idea of a Watch Night service, and it spread to other groups of Christians as a time of thanksgiving and rededication. But Watch Night had special significance to African slaves in the Confederate states on New Year's Eve in the year 1862 . . ."

Now a group of actors moved onto the stage at the front, all African-American members of SouledOut, adults, youth, and children, barefoot and dressed in rough and ragged clothing. They huddled together, except for Sherman Meeks, who stood, leaning on his cane. "Children!" His raspy voice quavered. "Pray tonight as n'er before. President Lincoln has issued an Emancipation Proclamation that all—I said *all*—slaves in the states of rebellion will be *free* by *law* at the stroke of midnight tonight!"

"Oh, bless Jesus!" one of the actors cried. I barely recognized Sherman's wife, Debra, a rag wrapped around her head, a soiled apron covering a shapeless dress.

"It's Freedom's Eve fo' sho'. Pray, children, that no hand will rise against this proclamation; nothing will stamp it out. Pray, children! Watch and pray!"

Those of us in our seats held our breath as the group huddled and prayed. Suddenly another barefoot teenager ran into the group, ringing a bell. "It's midnight," he cried. "We're free! Free!"

Now the crowd joined in the rejoicing, standing to our feet, shouting "Hallelujah!" and "Praise God!" along with the group on the platform. I sneaked a peek at Hakim's family sitting across the aisle from us. Even Geraldine Wilkins-Porter and her sister were clapping and smiling.

As all the lights came on and the "actors" disappeared, Pastor Cobbs took the mic. His face shone with sweat and he wiped it with a small towel. "Thanksgiving . . . Dedication . . . Freedom. Tonight we want to celebrate what a 'Watch Night' means in the twenty-first century as we, too, await a new year. First, our teens will help us reflect on the past year."

Curious, we all craned our necks as a group of the teens brought in several aluminum baking pans full of sand. They set a large pillar candle on a stool to one side and lit it. Beside the stool, they set a box of small, skinny candles. Then, one by one, several of the teens took a small candle, lit it, and gave a verbal thanksgiving before sticking the lit candle in the sand. "I thank God for my mom, who works two jobs so she can support us" . . . "Praise God I passed my PSAT test" . . . "I thank God that my dad stopped drinking . . ."

Pastor Cobbs then invited people from the congregation to come up and light a candle of thanks. Becky Wallace popped out of her seat, holding Little Andy by the hand. She lit a candle and stuck it in the sand. "I've got a whole long list to be thankful for, but mostly that God gave me a second chance to be a good mom to Little Andy."

She lit another candle for Andy. "And I'm thankful 'cause I got a racing car for Christmas! It goes real fast!" he shouted. Laughter broke open the dam—and for the next fifteen minutes candle after candle was lit, and thanksgivings offered to God for health, bills paid, friendships, family . . . and the candles set into the sand, blazing cheerfully.

"Look at all that praise!" Pastor Cobbs cried. "The world can't help but see our lights shining when we have a grateful heart." His deep baritone launched into a lively round of "This little light of mine! I'm gonna let it shine!" The congregation got to its feet again, clapping and singing our hearts out. From time to time, the front doors opened and a passerby slipped in to see what all the joy was about.

As the hands of the wall clock inched toward midnight, Pastor Clark joined Pastor Cobbs at the front—our Mutt-and-Jeff pastors, I used to say—urging us to sit once more. "We have a lot of young people with us tonight, praise God," Pastor Cobbs said. "I'd rather have them here tonight than out on the streets, getting drunk or high or shot—"

A chorus of "Amens!" and "Preach it, Pastor!" rang out.

"Young people, listen to me a moment. One hundred and thirty-three years ago, an enslaved people celebrated Freedom's Eve. *But Satan does not like a free people.* He is tempting you every way he can to make you a slave. I don't have to spell it out for you. Drugs, drinking, hookin' up, guns, gangbangin' . . . you know what I'm talking about. It looks glamorous for about a minute."

A few snickers rippled among the youth.

"But slavery comes with a high price, people! That kind of slavery puts young men in jail or in the morgue. That kind of slavery robs our beautiful girls of their precious virginity. They end up used and abused, with three babies and no daddy to provide for them. That kind of slavery leaves homes broken, kids with no one who cares. Life feels like a dead-end street. Some feel so hopeless they commit suicide."

He paused. The room was silent. Listening.

"There is only one true freedom, young man, young woman . . . and that is the freedom of forgiveness. Forgiveness that knows our sin and loves us anyway. Forgiveness that cancels the debt we owe. Forgiveness that gives us another chance to do it right—"

A movement across the aisle caught my eye. I turned slightly and saw Hakim leaning forward, looking my way. *"Thank you,"* he mouthed silently.

My eyes blurred.

"—That's what Christmas and Good Friday and Easter are all about," Pastor Cobbs was saying. "Jesus wants you to live! Jesus wants you to be free! He took the punishment for your sins so you wouldn't have to. That's forgiveness, and it's God's gift of love to you. Young man, young woman, make this a true Freedom's Eve . . . Let Jesus take all those lies Satan's telling you, all those bad choices, all the damage you are doing to your bodies—and exchange them for a clean heart and a second chance to live."

Pastor Cobbs walked back and forth, making eye contact. "If you want that kind of freedom, come on up here and let Pastor Clark and me pray with you. Don't be afraid. Don't be embarrassed. Coming up here is a small price to pray for freedom."

Several moments passed. Then a lanky teenage boy from the neighborhood who'd been coming to youth group lately walked to the front and knelt by the stubs of candles, still flickering. Then two girls. Another boy. And another. Pastor Clark and Pastor Cobbs began laying hands on the kneeling youth, praying, moving to the next.

Across the aisle, Hakim stood up.

My heart nearly stopped. *Oh, Jesus. Yes!* Why was I so shocked? Hadn't Nony said, *"God is at work, Jodi. I know it!"*

He walked to the front and sank to one knee. Denny slipped out of his seat and knelt beside Hakim, his arm around the boy's shoulder, praying for him. That's when the tears came.

As the prayers continued, Pastor Cobbs spoke once more into the mic. "I'd like all the youth to come forward so we can bless them. You adults, you come, too, and lay your hands on these young men and young women. Pray that God will bless them and that they will *be* a blessing in this new year. And as you pray, re-dedicate yourselves to be the man or woman, the mom or dad, the grandparent or mentor, the employer or employee, or the neighbor that God has called you to be."

The remaining young people and children joined the teens at

the altar, while a good many adults also came forward to stand behind them. I joined Denny behind Hakim and laid my hand on his shoulder. "Oh, God," Denny prayed, his voice joining dozens of others all around us. "Thank You for this beautiful young man! Pour out Your blessing on his life. You have redeemed him for a purpose—"

Someone else came up beside us and laid a hand on Hakim's shoulder. A manicured brown hand. At the same moment, I felt the person's arm go around my waist. I turned my head. Hakim's mother . . . and she was crying. I slipped my free arm around her waist, and we just stood together and cried.

22

𝓜idnight came and went. Outside, we heard the *poppity-pop-pop* of firecrackers going off, the big booms and sizzle-whistles of fireworks lighting up the sky, and somewhere the *crack! crack! crack!* of illegal gunfire. Church bells rang in the distance, and cars squealed through the shopping center parking lot with horns honking and stereos blaring, the *thump-thumpity-thump* of the bass notes so loud it rattled our windows.

But nothing could compare to the explosion of joy going off in my own spirit that night. It was truly "Freedom's Eve" . . . not just for a special eleven-year-old, though seeing Hakim at the altar was enough to make me want to shout. But I, too, had received the greatest of undeserved gifts: the forgiveness of Geraldine Wilkins-Porter.

If I doubted the significance of her embrace and the mingling of our tears, there was no doubt when we said good-bye. "You took one son away from me, Jodi Baxter," she whispered. "But you and God have given another son back to me. Thank you."

I could hardly sleep that night. My heart was so swollen with gratefulness to God, I wanted to put a praise CD on the player and dance all night. But I had to wait until Denny and Amanda got up. Patches and Peanuts, of course, thought praise dancing was a game invented just for them and kept attacking my stocking feet, getting stepped on and yowling in the process.

As far as I was concerned, we'd already had "church" . . . but New Year's Day fell on Sunday that year, so we dutifully attended the shortened worship service at SouledOut, rescheduled for eleven instead of ten. But I begged off from watching the Polar Bear swimmers jump in Lake Michigan this year. By now, it had become a tradition among the youth and young adults—and a few diehards like Denny who would probably jump in until they were sixty. But the Yada Yada reunion was at my house tonight . . . not to mention that yesterday had been Chanda's birthday, which we were going to celebrate along with everything else.

By the time the doorbell rang with the first arrivals, Denny had taken Amanda to a movie, the house smelled of pine cleaner, the kittens had been banished to Josh's soon-to-be guest bedroom, and I had a lemon Bundt cake chilling on the back porch. Candles flickered on every available ledge in the living and dining rooms, and Christmas carols on the CD player lent a festive air. With each new arrival, the holiday goodies multiplied, until the dining room table looked like an illustration for *Better Homes and Gardens* magazine . . . or a warning ad about bad cholesterol.

Then I noticed something. Nonyameko was wearing a casual red dashiki with black-and-white embroidery around the neck and sleeves, almost a unisex African style. Hoshi had on a T-shaped cotton robe of indigo blue, with wide sleeves and a cloth belt, telling someone it was a Japanese *yukata*. Chanda's turquoise Jamaican beach dress hung from her shoulders to her ankles, but had slits up to her midthigh.

I elbowed Stu, who was wearing designer jeans, boots, and her red beret. "I thought we weren't going to get decked out for this party."

"Didn't you see the e-mail I sent yesterday? The committee said it's optional, but if anyone wanted to wear something representing her ethnic background or just something that says 'this is me,' we said go for it."

"Oh, great. What am I supposed to wear? A loaf of Wonder Bread on my head?"

Stu cracked up. "Don't worry about it, Jodi. That apron you're wearing will do. Or stick a pencil in your hair. Isn't that what teachers do?"

I looked down. *Sheesh*. I'd forgotten to take off the dirty apron I'd been wearing all afternoon. I whipped it off . . . and found myself grinning. I could always clothe myself with "compassion and kindness," like the scripture I'd read at Josh and Edesa's wedding.

I had to admit, it was fun to see what people were wearing. Yo-Yo did what came naturally, wearing her favorite wheat-denim overalls. Becky Wallace—so gauche it was funny—came in a pair of tight jeans, tank top, jean jacket, wraparound sunglasses, and red bandana, similar to the one she'd been wearing when we first "met" her, to use the term loosely. High on heroin, she had burst into my house, robbed the prayer group at knifepoint, earning the name "Bandana Woman" . . . until God showed us she was a hurting person too.

Several sisters just wore their favorite, comfy clothes—a velour pants-and-top outfit for Avis, jeans for Florida, a roomy caftan Estelle had sewn for herself.

Ruth, however, came wearing a traditional Jewish *snood* made of soft, burgundy-colored velveteen, snug around her face but loose in the back, like a little bag covering her hair. "Three words describe all Jewish clothing," she sniffed. "Modesty, modesty, modesty."

Edesa and Delores wore brightly colored shawls from their respective countries. Delores's was long—a *rebozo*, she called it. "Very useful for cradling a *bambino* on your hip. I'm giving it to Edesa after tonight."

"I'll take it!" Edesa laughed. "But this"—she twirled in the fringed black shawl with the red roses she'd worn the night Josh had given her an engagement ring—"is for dancing!"

"Well, then, let's get this party started!" Avis turned off the CD player and began to sing an *a cappella* chorus of "What a Mighty God We Serve!" It was impossible to sit down while singing *"Angels bow before Him, heaven and earth adore Him,"* so we stood and clapped and lifted our hands in praise. As one song ended, someone else started another. We filled the room with "The Joy of the Lord Is Our Strength"; the spiritual, "Soon and Very Soon"; and "The Name of the Lord Is a Strong Tower."

We finally fell into our seats, laughing and fanning ourselves. "Oh, sisters," Nonyameko said, her smile large and her eyes bright with happy tears. "You do not know how much it means to me, to be worshiping and singing with my Yada Yada sisters once more. Oh, praise to the One who gives us a *new* song."

"Amen to that!" Florida said. "But I need me some water, or the next song just gonna be a big croak."

I hustled into the kitchen to get a pitcher of cold water and some paper cups. By the time I got back, someone had suggested we do our gift exchange to our Secret Sisters. "Aw," I said, pouring water. "That's the first time we've had gifts under the tree this year. I'd kind of like to look at them a while longer . . . okay, okay, just kidding."

Edesa looked at me oddly. When I handed her some water, she whispered, "You feel badly, Jodi? About no Christmas gifts this year because of the wedding?"

I set down the pitcher and hugged her tight. "Oh, Edesa," I whispered in her ear. "*You* are the best Christmas gift our family ever had. I'm sorry I said something so silly."

"So how do we do this thang?" Florida was saying. "Hand 'em out all at once?"

"No, no, no," Stu protested. "Here, let's start with the beginning of the alphabet . . . that would be Adele. Adele, you give your gift to your Secret Sister, then she'll give her gift to her Secret Sister, and we'll just keep on like that. The person who gets a gift will be the next one to give one, got it?"

"All right." Adele huffed to her feet, plucked a square envelope out of the tree branches, waved it a few times . . . and handed it to me.

I wanted to laugh. Adele got *my* name, and I got hers? Too funny. But I opened my envelope and pulled out a gift certificate from Adele's Hair and Nails. "'To Jodi Baxter,'" I read. "'Good for the following . . . ' Whoa! She has hair color, haircut, hair set and brush-out, manicure, *and* spa pedicure all checked. Wahoo!" I waved it in the air, then jumped up to hug Adele. "Thanks, Adele!" I put a finger to her lips. "Now, don't you dare say how much I need all this!"

Everybody laughed.

I went to the tree and picked up my wrapped package. "Stu had a good idea for keeping our gift exchange moving, but . . . sorry. *My* Secret Sister is Adele, so the loop ends here." I handed Adele the package. "Merry Christmas."

Adele unwrapped the square box I'd used to disguise what was inside. "A candle," she mused, reading the box. "How nice." She started to set it aside.

"Open it, you ninny!" I said. "Don't trust the box."

She opened the box . . . and pulled out the necklace I'd made. She looked at it a long moment, then smiled, showing the little gap between her front teeth. "MaDear's buttons," she murmured. "I love it. Yes, I do." She slipped it over her head, which was easy because I'd strung the multicolored buttons of all sizes and shapes on a stretchy cord. "Thanks, Jodi." She seemed a little overcome.

Stu took over. "Okay, we have to start the loop again. Avis, you're the next A."

Avis picked up the largest package under the tree, which seemed rather heavy, and handed it to Delores. "It's not very personal," she apologized. "In fact, I was thinking mostly of your kids, but . . . "

Delores opened the package. Her eyes widened. "A laptop computer? But Avis, that's too much!"

"Don't worry, Delores. I, um, didn't exactly pay for it. Peter upgraded his laptop, even though this one is perfectly good." She rolled her eyes. "That's what happens when you're married to a computer geek. He's got to have the latest bells and whistles."

Delores shook her head happily. "Oh! Ricardo and I have been praying about getting a computer for the kids, to do their homework, to keep up with school. This is an answer to prayer! *Gloria a*

Dios!" She clapped her hands. "Now, it is my turn." She retrieved a flat package from under the tree and handed it to Hoshi.

Hoshi eagerly opened the gift, pulling out an oblong white cotton cloth edged in lace, which looked as if it could decorate the center of a table or dresser top. Something had been embroidered around the inner edges. "*Sister* and *Friend* in English," Hoshi murmured, turning the cloth. "Then *Hermana* and *Amiga* in Spanish. Then . . . " Her eyes widened. "It is here in Japanese too!" She held up the cloth, and we all saw the Japanese word symbols, completely unintelligible to the rest of us.

"Did I get it right?" Delores made a hopeful grimace.

"Exactly right, my sister and my friend." Hoshi gave Delores a warm hug.

Then it was Hoshi's turn. She presented a book about origami to Yo-Yo, along with squares of brightly colored paper. "Cool!" Yo-Yo said. "You mean, this will tell me how to make them cool birds and frogs and things you made for Nony that time?"

But once she'd admired the book, Yo-Yo got very quiet. "Yo-Yo?" Stu prodded. "Your turn."

"Yeah. I know. But . . . well, I got Chanda's name. And . . ." Yo-Yo suddenly threw out her arms in frustration. "Chanda, ya already got everything money can buy! And I ain't good at no sewing or handmade stuff. So, well, I . . . " She withdrew a crumpled envelope from her overall pocket. "Here. There's twenty bucks inside. I thought maybe you and me could go to the movies together sometime. You know, *do* something."

Chanda's face broke wide with delight. "*Irie, mon!* One ting money can't buy is just spending time wit' me friends. So, now. Do you get to pick de movie or mi? You free next Saturday?"

Everyone clapped and hooted. A grin replaced Yo-Yo's anxious frown.

"Now mi!" Chanda fished a classy blue envelope out of the Christmas tree. "God been talkin' to mi 'bout money, dat it's too easy to give money wit'out giving miself. So, dis is for Ruth."

Ruth sighed. "Just my luck. I could have used a million dollars or so." She opened the envelope, then laughed. "But *this* I can use." She read the handmade gift certificate. "'This certificate is good for one day at the zoo with Havah and Isaac.' And what's this?" She pulled out a fifty-dollar bill.

"Dat's for you and Ben to go out to dinner while *we* chasing your kids at de zoo!"

The rest of the gifts were exchanged with laughter, hugs, and a few tears. Ruth gave Nony a framed picture of all us Yadas that Ben had taken at Edesa's wedding—and ended up having to promise she'd get copies for all the rest of us too . . . Nony gave Florida a CD of South African worship music . . . Florida gave Edesa a coupon booklet that had been filled in with things like *"Babysit Gracie"* (there were a lot of those), *"Free advice"* (that got a laugh), *"Instant quiet if the boys play their music too loud"* ("Oh, you'll need that one!" Becky Wallace said, rolling her eyes), and *"Hugs on demand."* . . . Edesa gave Estelle a scroll tied with a ribbon that promised private Spanish lessons. "You will get many more jobs for elder care if you can speak some Spanish," Edesa said knowingly . . . Estelle had sewn a set of kitchen curtains for Becky's new apartment, rendering Becky speechless . . . Becky gave Stu a certificate good for six hours of housecleaning, to be used in whatever combination Stu wanted. "That's to make up for all the times I drove you nuts leavin' dirty dishes in the sink and leavin' my wet towels on the bathroom floor."

There was only one gift left under the tree. Stu retrieved it and stood in front of Avis. "Well. I think it is very appropriate that Avis should be the final one to receive a gift. Last but not least, you know. As our fearless leader, the one who has kept us all in line and forged a path for us to follow, our elder stateswoman—"

"Oh, stop." Avis rolled her eyes.

Stu, barely concealing a grin, handed her the gaily wrapped package. Avis opened it and pulled out a large pink T-shirt. And then she started to laugh. "Oh! Stu, you didn't! Where am I going to wear *this*?"

"What? Show us!" we all cried.

Avis turned the T-shirt around. It read in fancy script: *"I'm too Sexy to be Fifty."*

At that point, we all lost it. Amid hoots and laughter, we threw out suggestions: "To school, of course!" . . . "Could be a nightshirt." . . . "Peter will like it!" . . . "Wear it to embarrass your kids." Still laughing, we finally broke for refreshments and to let Chanda cut her lemon birthday cake.

Thirty minutes later, as the others headed back toward the living room to begin our sharing and prayer time, I blew out the dining room candles that were drowning in their own wax, checked on Patches and Peanut in Josh's old bedroom (cuddled together in a pile of black, white, and orange fur), and refilled the pitcher of ice water. Padding silently down the hall with the pitcher, I stopped in the living room archway. Nonyameko was sharing with the rest of the sisters what she had already told me at the Heartland Café, the sorrows and joys of the pathway God had placed before her and Mark . . .

That's it, isn't it, Lord? A pathway with both sorrow and joy.

My eyes caressed the heads of all my Yada Yada sisters listening intently to Nony's story. Each one had a story—a story that was only beginning, whether it was twenty-something Yo-Yo, worried about the half brothers she'd been raising since she was a teenager, or Ruth, becoming a mother for the first time at fifty! Of twins!

Oh, the challenges each one in that room faced! Yet each one had so much to give. Hoshi, bless her, wanted to give back to international students what she'd been given—friendship and a new life in Jesus. Estelle, who came to us from Manna House, wasn't exactly a spring chicken, and yet she had such a heart to care for the homebound elderly.

As I looked at each face around the circle, I realized just how much each one had already given, not only to this group, not only to others . . . but to me.

My eyes blurred. *Thank You, Jesus! Thank You for giving Yada Yada to me as companions on this journey of faith—*

Well, you were a hard nut to crack, Jodi Baxter, said the Voice in my spirit. *Religious types always are. You needed sisters like Florida and Yo-Yo and Adele to break through the churchy facade that stood between Me and you.*

Yeah, I know.

But I need to ask you something, Jodi. God's Spirit was gentle, but insistent. *What if I send all of these sisters to serve Me elsewhere, and they're not here to prop you up? What will you do then?*

I didn't want to think about that. But for some reason, I wasn't afraid. *I don't know . . . but I know I can trust You, Lord. I have Your Word to guide me, and You've given me the weapons of praise and prayer.*

That's right, Jodi. Even though friends and family may leave you, I will never leave you nor forsake you. That's a promise.

"Hey, Jodi! Put down that pitcher and come join us. We're going to lay hands on Nony and pray for her before we hear from the rest."

I obeyed, joy pushing a smile onto my face. For this evening, this moment, my heart and this house was full. And the Yada Yada Prayer Group was doing what we did best . . .

Pray.

A note from the author:

This novella marks the end of the Yada Yada series. I never imagined it would be more than one novel, much less seven! It has certainly been a life-changing journey for me. God has taught me so much in the writing. Sometimes I felt as if I were on a roller coaster, just hanging on for the ride! Thank you, faithful sister-friends, for sharing the journey with me. I'd love to hear what it's meant for you. You can contact me through our website: www.daveneta.com. God BLESS you!

Sincerely,

Neta

P.S. But just in case you're wondering . . . Yes, I'm working on a new series (due to premier in Spring 2009) with a cast of new characters. But remember the old camp song, "Make new friends, but keep the old . . ."? You'll find some of your old Yada Yada friends woven into the new series too! Visit my website to sign up for updates. See you next time around.

Reading Group Guide

1. The Yada Yada Prayer Group wants to celebrate and get "decked out"—nothing wrong with that! When was the last time you really got "decked out"? What do you consider the joys and pitfalls of getting "decked out"?

2. Besides weddings, anniversaries, graduations, and birthdays, what are some *other* events or milestones (often overlooked) that deserve celebration?

3. The Manna House women's shelter provides a backdrop for much of this story. Have you ever volunteered at a shelter or food pantry for those without basic necessities? Share your experience. In what ways did volunteering change *you*?

4. Jodi found "Mr. Tallahassee" (Amanda's schoolmate) extremely annoying, but God told her to sow seeds of friendship anyway. Are your children's friends welcome at your house—whether they are five, fifteen, or twenty-five? How could you make your home more hospitable toward guests of all ages?

5. When Jodi realized she knew one of the youths who snatched her purse, do you think she did the right thing by *not* reporting it to the police? Why or why not?

6. How do you feel about Edesa's decision to keep Carmelita's orphaned child, even though she and Josh weren't married yet? What risks was she taking?

7. Josh told his parents God used the story of Joseph to speak to him about marrying Edesa *now* and accepting the child too. Has a story from the Bible ever spoken to your specific circumstances? In what way?

8. Why do you think Josh and Edesa chose Colossians 3:12–14 for their wedding scripture? In what way might these verses rearrange our priorities as women?

9. Jodi decides the unpolished Christmas play at the Manna House shelter and its cast of Katrina evacuees and down-on-their-luck residents is actually very appropriate. Today's version of the Christmas story (complete with music and candlelight and glittering decorations) shields us from its poverty-stricken setting and common characters: an out-of-wedlock pregnancy, a hurry-up wedding, a travel-weary couple without room reservations, a destitute baby born in a barn. If the Son of God were born *today*, what might be the equivalent for the town of Bethlehem? . . . the stable? . . . the shepherds who got the first announcement? (Who would believe and come running?)

10. In a way, the story of Hakim and Jodi provides "bookends" to the Yada Yada series. Why do you think Hakim responded to

the invitation to make this truly "Freedom's Eve"? What did this mean for Jodi? For Hakim's mother?

11. How do you usually celebrate New Year's Eve? How might you add meaning to this holiday with ideas from this novel?

12. In your journey with the Yada Yada Prayer Group, what has meant the most to you? What have you learned about prayer? ... about worship? ... about the "other" members of the body of Christ who are different from yourself?

Celebrate!

If you're like Jodi Baxter (it's a little scary how many other "Jodies" are out there!), it probably feels as if you've barely recovered from the last holiday season—paid the bills . . . put away the decorations . . . discovered the forgotten wrapping paper still under the bed—when the holidays loom large on the calendar again.

Hopefully it won't take a sprained ankle to slow you down long enough to think about how you want to celebrate the holiday season this year.

Of course, if you want fancy decorating tips, last-minute gift ideas, or tantalizing menus for a seven-course meal, feel free to pick up one of the slick women's magazines at the grocery store checkout, take a few guilt trips that you're not doing enough . . . then go back to "doing the holidays" the same old way.

But if you'd like a few tips on celebrating the holiday season "the Yada Yada Way," sit tight and take a bite!

Celebrate Thanksgiving

Thanksgiving! *Giving thanks* . . . that's what this holiday is about. Families getting together. And food, of course. Lots and lots of food. Most every family has their favorite foods and recipes, from the traditional turkey (*and* ham *and* macaroni and cheese, staples at most African-American Thanksgiving tables) to pumpkin pie (or sweet potato pie). But before you dive in, it's worth taking a few minutes to reflect on the historical aspects of this day.

Reflect

The following account of the "First Thanksgiving" in the New World provides a meaningful context. However, the Native American corn mentioned here was not popcorn, nor would it have been very suitable for eating on the cob. It was primarily ground for meal.

> Our [wheat] did prove well, and God be praised, we had a good increase of Indian corn, and our barley indifferent good, but our peas not worth the gathering, for we feared they were too late sown. They came up very well, and blossomed, but the sun parched them in the blossom. Our harvest being gotten in, our governor sent four men [out] fowling, . . . so we might . . . rejoice together after we had gathered the fruit of our labors.
>
> They . . . in one day killed as much fowl as, with a little help beside, served the company almost a week. At which time, amongst other recreations, . . . many of the Indians [came] amongst us, [including] their greatest king Massasoit, with some ninety men, whom for three days we entertained and feasted. And they went out and killed five deer, which they brought to the plantation and bestowed on our governor, and upon the captain and others.
>
> And although it be not always so plentiful as it was at this time with us, yet by the goodness of God, we are so far from want that we often wish you partakers of our plenty.[1]

222

It's also worth noting that a "thanksgiving day" is not a uniquely American holiday. Here are some other countries that have also set aside days to give thanks.

Other Countries' Days of Thanksgiving Celebrations

- **Brazil,** *Dia Nacional de Acao de Gracas*, fourth Thursday of November.
- **British Isles,** Lammas Day, a harvest festival.
- **Canada,** Thanksgiving Day or *Fete de Grace*, or Harvest Home Festival, second Monday in October.
- **Germany,** *Erntedankfest*, first Sunday in October.
- **Israel,** *Sukkot*, Feast of Booths, the fifth day after Yom Kippur.
- **Japan,** Labor Thanksgiving Day, November 23.
- **Korea,** *Chusok*, fifteenth day of the eighth lunar month of the traditional Korean calendar.
- **Liberia,** Thanksgiving Day, first Thursday in November.
- **Mexico,** Independence Day, September 16.
- **Switzerland,** The Federal Day of Thanks, Penance, and Prayer, third Sunday in September.

Give Thanks!

However you celebrate this day, *don't forget to give thanks.* God's blessings are so freely given and so abundant. But it's not "*what* we have" so much as "*how* we have it" that give us reason to celebrate with joy and thanksgiving.

- Consider this proverb: "Better a little with the fear of the LORD than great wealth with turmoil. Better a meal of vegetables where there is love than a fattened calf with hatred" (Proverbs 15:16–17 NIV).

- Discuss with your family members: "What do you think this proverb means for *our* family? Are we focusing too much on our problems and not enough on our blessings? Are there family quarrels that need to be mended so we can truly give thanks?"

Expand Your Table

- The whole family is coming for Thanksgiving? Great! But consider adding a few international students from the local college, a few singles from church, or the older couple down the street whose children live in distant states.
- At the first Thanksgiving in 1621, Native Americans and European immigrants sat down at the same table and broke bread together. Why not invite a family from a culture or ethnic group different from your own to share Thanksgiving Day with your family? Let each family bring traditional dishes from their own culture. Listen to one another's stories. It will be a Thanksgiving Day you will never forget.
- The family can't come this year? Quit moping! Volunteer to serve Thanksgiving dinner at a local homeless shelter, soup kitchen, or other ministry that serves the elderly, the lonely, or the poor. Don't just dish out food. Sit and talk with the guests. Play checkers or cards. You will not only be a blessing, but you will be blessed!

A Thanksgiving Mural

- Tack a long piece of newsprint or a large poster board somewhere near the Thanksgiving table with colorful markers nearby. Encourage family and guests to write their thanksgivings on the mural during the day—no limit! Little ones can draw pictures. Date the mural and save it until the following year . . . then bring it out for everyone to enjoy before starting a new one.

Popcorn Praise
- Before serving the food at your Thanksgiving dinner, place three kernels of popcorn on each dinner plate, then pass around a bowl, inviting each person to tell three things he or she is thankful for as they place their kernels in the bowl. You might assist younger children by suggesting categories: family, God, something fun.
- Or . . . pass the bowl at three different times during the meal—before it begins, during the meal, when it's time for dessert. Pick a theme for the thanksgivings each time: "Something that happened this past year" . . . "Why you are thankful for the person sitting next to you" . . . "Something you are looking forward to" . . . etc.

A Family Advent Celebration

Like Jodi Baxter, you may sometimes feel pushed into Christmas by the frenzy and commercialism of the season without a moment to consider the magnitude of God being born on earth to live among us. For centuries, many Christians have slowed their hectic lives during the four weeks before Christmas to focus on the reason for the season by celebrating Advent—a word that means "coming" or "arriving"—a time of reflecting on Israel's long wait for a Messiah in order to prepare ourselves to celebrate His coming. Because of its ancient origin, there are many variations in the tradition, but "Ready My Heart," a simple carol by Lois Shuford, captures the essence well.

Ready my heart for the birth of Emmanuel
Ready my soul for the Prince of Peace.
Heap the straw of my life for His body to lie on,
Light the candle of hope. Let the Child come in.
    Alleluia, Alleluia,
    Alleluia, Christ the Savior is born![2]

The Advent Wreath

- In the center of your table, construct a wreath of evergreens or holly. (Artificial greens or a wreath of ceramic or wood is less flammable.) Evenly space four purple or red candles in holders around the perimeter. In the center of the wreath, place a large white candle that is one and a half to three inches in diameter.

- Traditionally, *purple* has been a color that reminds us of sorrow and repentance, but it is also the color of royalty. The *evergreens* remind us of the eternal life Jesus Christ brings as His gift to us. The glow from all the *candles* reminds us that Jesus is the Light of the World.

- The first candle is often called the *Prophets' Candle* and is meant to signify the hope of Messiah. The second is the *Bethlehem Candle*, reminding us that God came in a humble manner. The third candle (sometimes pink to express joy) is the *Shepherds' Candle.* The fourth candle is the *Angels' Candle,* symbolizing the good news of peace they brought. The white candle is the *Christ Candle* to be lit on Christmas Eve or Christmas Day.

Celebrating Advent

- Advent begins four Sundays before Christmas (usually the first Sunday after Thanksgiving).
- *On the first Sunday,* do the full celebration (see "A Family Advent Celebration") for that week together as a family. Repeat the Call and Response, read the first week's scripture, light the first candle while saying its meaning and allowing it to burn during your meal, and sing the first verse of "O Come, O Come, Emmanuel." During the week, do an abbreviated version: Light the first candle each night while repeating its meaning, and sing the first verse of "O Come, O Come, Emmanuel."
- On the *second, third, and fourth Sundays of Advent,* do that week's full celebration, adding the second, third, and fourth candle lightings as appropriate. On the weekdays of those weeks, do the shortened version of lighting all candles to date while saying their meanings, but sing only that week's verse of "O Come, O Come, Emmanuel."
- Each Scripture passage is read only on its respective Sunday. The lighting of the candles, however, is added accumulatively until all the candles are burning together the fourth week and on Christmas.

A Family Advent Celebration

First Week
- **Call and Response**
  LEADER: *The people who walked in darkness have seen a great light.*
  ALL: *Those who dwelled in a land of deep darkness, on them has light shined.*
  LEADER: *For unto us a child is born, unto us a son is given, and the government shall be upon his shoulders.*
  ALL: *And his name shall be called Wonderful Counselor, Mighty God, Everlasting Father, Prince of Peace.*
- **Read the first scripture:** Isaiah 40:1–5.
- **Light the first candle,** and say:
  > *I light this candle in memory of God's promise to send a Savior who will forgive our sin and deliver us from injustice.*
- **Sing** the first verse and refrain of "O Come, O Come, Emmanuel."

Second Week
- **Call and Response**—repeat from the first week.
- **Light the first candle,** repeat its meaning, and sing the first verse and refrain of "O Come, O Come, Emmanuel."
- **Read the second scripture:** John 8:12.
- **Light the second candle,** and say:
  > *I light this candle in memory of Jesus Christ, who is the Light of the World.*
- **Sing** the second verse and refrain of "O Come, O Come, Emmanuel."

Third Week
- **Call and Response**—repeat from the first week.
- **Light the first and second candles,** repeat their meanings, and sing the respective verses of "O Come, O Come, Emmanuel."
- **Read the third scripture:** Luke 1:32–33.
- **Light the third candle,** and say:

  I light this candle in memory of Jesus, born of the house of David, in the town of Bethlehem.
- **Sing** the third verse and refrain of "O Come, O Come, Emmanuel."

Fourth Week
- **Call and Response**—repeat from the first week.
- **Light the first three candles,** repeat their meanings, and sing the respective verses of "O Come, O Come, Emmanuel."
- **Read the fourth scripture:** Revelation 5:9–10
- **Light the fourth candle,** and say:

  I light this candle for Jesus Christ, who was born to be Lord of the nations.
- **Sing** the fourth verse and refrain of "O Come, O Come, Emmanuel."

Christmas Day
- **Call and Response**—repeat from the first week.
- **Light the first four candles,** repeating their meanings, and sing the respective verses of "O Come, O Come, Emmanuel."
- **Read the Christmas scripture:** Luke 2:1–20.
- **Light the Christmas candle.** Say:

I light this candle for Jesus Christ, who was born in a manger on Christmas Day.

- **Sing** "Away in a Manger."

Suggestions:

- Doing the celebration each day will undoubtedly use up your candles, but the daily meditation can be meaningful, so just replace the candles with new ones.
- Let each child and/or parent be responsible for lighting one particular candle and saying what it means (e.g., oldest child lights first candle, second child second candle, a parent lights third candle, etc.).
- If the full Advent celebration is too long for your family, just read the new scripture and light the new candle each week.

O Come, O Come, Emmanuel

1. *O come, O come, Emmanuel,*
And ransom captive Israel,
That mourns in lonely exile here,
Until the Son of God appears.

Refrain:
Rejoice! Rejoice! Emmanuel
Shall come to thee, O Israel!

2. *O come, Thou Dayspring, come and cheer*
Our spirits by Thine advent here;
Disperse the gloomy clouds of night,
And death's dark shadows put to flight.

3. O come, Thou Key of David, come
And open wide our heavenly home.
Make safe the way that leads on high,
And close the path to misery.

4. O come, Desire of nations, bind
All peoples in one heart and mind.
Bid envy, strife, and quarrels cease.
Fill the whole world with heaven's peace.[3]

Celebrate a New Year's Eve "Watch Night"

New Year's Eve! The beginning of a New Year is celebrated all over our globe—though not all countries celebrate on December 31. China and Israel, for example, have calendars based on a lunar month, so the date of their New Year celebrations, while consistent on a lunar calendar, change on the "standard" solar calendar most of us use.

Many of us remember the New Year's Eve not too long ago when the calendar flipped from 1999 to 2000—the second millennium was here! Wahoo! What an historical event! (Though, to be honest, the next day pretty much resembled the one just before it. The sun rose, the sun set, in that wonderful rhythm of God's awesome creation.)

Reflect

Undoubtedly, people have commemorated New Year's Eve ever since primitive calendars were able to identify the date. But Christian "Watch Night" services seem to have begun with the

Moravians, a small community of believers in Bohemia (now the Czech Republic) in the eighteenth century. These Christians, persecuted because of their protests against a state church and its many excesses, fled to Bohemia and eventually to the New World in search of freedom to worship God according to the New Testament model. In 1733, they held their first Watch Night service, a time to give thanks to God for His blessing and protection in the year past, and to rededicate themselves to God's service in the coming year.

John Wesley borrowed the idea for his followers, who were later known as Methodists. Since then, many modern Christians have observed some sort of New Year's Eve service reflecting on God's goodness during the past year and recommitting themselves to Him for the New Year. Two biblical themes are often emphasized: Jesus' words before His betrayal, "*Watch and pray* so that you will not fall into temptation" (Matthew 26:41 NIV; emphasis added), and His warning to be ready for His return at the end of the age, "Therefore *keep watch*, because you do not know the day or the hour" (Matthew 25:13 NIV; emphasis added).

However, African-American Christians experienced special significance in this observance on the night of December 31, 1862, which for them was also "Freedom's Eve"—the night before the Emancipation Proclamation went into effect and all the slaves in the Confederate states were declared free. As they came together in churches and private homes all across the nation, hope, fear, and prayers gave way to shouts of joy, songs, and thanksgiving to God when word spread after midnight that the Proclamation had not been retracted. It's an event that all Christians can incorporate into their Watch Night services, praising God for bringing us through another year and thanking Him for both physical and spiritual freedom.

A Watch Night Celebration

If your usual New Year's Eve consists of sacking out in front of the TV and watching "the ball" fall in Times Square . . . or leaving the kids with a babysitter while you hold a glass of bubbly and sing "Auld Lang Syne" at the office party . . . consider celebrating a family-friendly Watch Night. The following Watch Night celebration can be adapted for use in a church setting, or at home with family and friends.

Invite!

- "Make new friends, but keep the old . . . " the old camp song goes. A New Year's Eve celebration is an excellent time to celebrate "old friends" and "new." A youth group from one church could invite a youth group from another church. A family could invite another family—or two! One "old friends" and one "new."
- It's important to keep our children's hearts—and our own—open to those Jesus loves but who are often overlooked. "Birds of a feather flock together" is *not* in the Bible!

Eat!

- Begin the evening with a potluck meal. If your church or neighborhood involves many nationalities, this could be an "international night" with foods from different countries.
- If done at home with family and friends, plan a festive meal for which various participants help prepare different dishes.

Play!

- After the meal, play games that adults and youth can play together—relays, guessing games, icebreakers.

- Play charades . . . but instead of using the traditional categories of book title, movie title, song, etc., pantomime events with which everyone is familiar from the preceding year. Agree on categories such as *Happy Event* (demonstrated by pulling one's mouth into a grin with fingers), *Sad Event* (pull mouth down into a frown), *Crazy Event* (circling fingers around ears), *Scary Event* (holding eyes exceptionally wide with hands), *God's Provision* (fingers raked down over one's head like falling rain), etc. Other gestures may follow the game's typical sign language. (Google "charades" on the Internet for examples.) No words or sounds may be spoken. No letters may be "drawn" in the air to spell out a word. Rather than dividing into teams, each player can take a turn portraying an event while everyone else guesses. Little ones may need an adult's help.

Reflect!
- Before midnight arrives, explain some of the background of Watch Night services as mentioned earlier in the "Reflect" section. Read Mark 13:28–37, in which Jesus told how we can recognize when the time for His return is approaching and encouraged us to be ready by watching and praying. (You may want to use the King James Version, which uses that language.)

Sing!
- Sing songs about God's faithfulness, either from a hymnal or some of the contemporary praise and worship songs.

Commit!

- Invite individuals to renew their commitment to the Lord as they prepare to enter the New Year. This could be a spontaneously worded commitment with a particular focus, or, for the younger ones, it might reiterate these words from Joshua 24:15: "But as for me and my household, we will serve the Lord" (NIV).

- As each person makes a commitment, let him or her light a candle and put it in a candleholder on a table or plant it in a bed of sand in a large pan. The more candles, the brighter the light.

Bless!

- An alternative (or an addition) might be to pray blessings on the children and teenagers as the parents light a candle for each one. For inspiration, read Mark 10:13–16, imagining what Jesus might have said as He took the children into His arms, placed His hands on their heads, and blessed them.

Ring in the New Year!

- At midnight, ring in the New Year by letting everyone ring a bell, jingle keys, shake a tambourine, or tap lightly on a glass with a spoon.

- Conclude the evening by singing "This Little Light of Mine." Sing all the usual verses and make up your own: *"All around my neighborhood/ With all my friends/ Every day in school/ When I go to work,* etc. . . . *I'm going to let it shine! Let it shine, let it shine, let it shine!"*

Jodi's Hungarian Chicken and Dumplings

Jodi's not Hungarian, but who cares? It's all that paprika! When the weather gets cold, the Baxter clan starts clamoring for chicken and dumplings, the perfect cold-weather comfort food.

1 chicken, cut up, or eight pieces
1 tbsp. paprika
$^1/_2$ tsp. salt
$^1/_4$ tsp. black pepper
$^1/_2$ tsp. dried thyme
1 tbsp. olive oil
2 stalks of celery, split and cut into 3 inch pieces
4 med. carrots, split and cut into 3 inch pieces
2 med. onions, quartered
4 cups of chicken stock (or dissolve 2 tbsp. bouillon in water)

Rinse the chicken, pat dry, and cover with the paprika, salt, pepper, and thyme, rubbing it in. Sauté the chicken in the oil until brown (about 15 minutes).

(Recipe continues on next page.)

Add the vegetables and chicken to the chicken stock and bring it to a boil in a large pot. Simmer for about 30 minutes.

Don't get sidetracked by the phone or the newspaper. You still have to . . .

Make the dumplings:
1 ½ cups unbleached flour
1 ½ tsp. baking powder
¼ tsp. salt
3 tbsp. chopped fresh parsley (or 3 tsp. dried)
2 tbsp. solid vegetable shortening
½ cup milk

Combine ingredients (reserving some parsley for a garnish) and form into golf-ball-sized dumplings. Drop the dumplings into the simmering broth, arranging them so they will expand to cover the surface. Put a lid on your pot and cook for another 15 minutes.

Garnish with reserved parsley and serve in bowls to accommodate the juice. Makes 4 to 6 servings—but don't count on any leftovers.

Consider coleslaw or cucumber salad as a side.

Estelle's Orange-Smothered Pork Chops

Don't tell anybody, but Estelle accidentally invented this when she had a dab of marmalade she didn't have the heart to throw out, so she threw it on the pork chop she was cooking instead. It was so good, she keeps a jar of marmalade now just for chops.

One pork chop per person (select chops about $1/2$ inch thick)
Corn oil
1 tbsp. orange marmalade per chop
$1/4$ cup orange juice per chop
Pinch of ground, rubbed sage per chop
A couple dashes of seasoned salt per chop
Freshly ground black pepper to taste

In a skillet large enough to accommodate your chops flat on the bottom, put about 1 tbsp. of corn oil. (More may be required if your chops are particularly lean.)

Cover each chop with the seasoned salt, sage, and pepper.

Sear the chops in the skillet over high heat until brown on both sides. Pour off excess grease and allow the pan to cool slightly. Mix the marmalade into the orange juice and pour over chops. Increase heat and gently simmer for about 20 minutes or until the orange juice thickens to a syrup, turning the chops 2 or 3 times. Do not allow the syrup to scorch.

Serve on a bed of rice, pouring the juice over the top. Garnish with sprigs of fresh, curly parsley. *(And it's okay to puff out your chest and whisper, "Secret recipe," when your family raves. Estelle won't mind.)*

Estelle's Holiday Corn Puddin'

"Corn pudding?! Never heard of it!" Just smile smugly and tell them Estelle guarantees this will melt in their mouths. It looks pretty, too, with those bits of red and green peppers.

1 can (15 oz.) of creamed corn
3 tbsp. flour
1 tsp. salt
1 tbsp. sugar
2 dashes nutmeg
2 dashes black pepper
3 eggs, beaten well
3 tbsp. melted butter
1 cup milk (for richer flavor, try soy milk)
$1/4$ green bell pepper, finely diced
$1/4$ red bell pepper, finely diced
Paprika

Preheat oven to 325 degrees. Combine creamed corn and all dry ingredients, mixing well. Stir in the eggs, butter, and milk. Add the peppers, and pour all ingredients into a greased $1^1/_2$-quart baking dish. Sprinkle the top with paprika and bake for 1 hour or until the pudding is firm and a knife comes out clean. Serves 4 to 6.

Jodi's Flaky Piecrust

Jodi says, "Can't knit . . . can't skydive . . . can't dance the light fantastic. But I can make a good piecrust." Denny likes to make her prove it (he has a weakness for pie).

Jodi's hint: a piecrust that flakes like good pastry is as much technique as the right ingredients.

2 cups flour
1 tsp. salt
$^2/_3$ cup vegetable shortening, divided
 • cut $^1/_3$ cup shortening into dry ingredients with a pastry blender until well blended
 • cut in remaining $^1/_3$ cup shortening
5 to 7 tbsp. ice water (fill a small bowl with ice cubes, then add water)

Sprinkle 1 tbsp. of ice water at a time onto the flour/shortening mixture while you toss it with a fork. Add from 5 to 7 spoonfuls . . . just until dough can be gathered into a ball.

Divide dough, slightly more than half for the bottom crust. Roll out dough quickly and gently on a floured counter or board. (Too much handling is what makes it tough.) Pat any tears with a dab of water to stick the dough back together.

Turn over once. Dust with flour as needed to roll smoothly to a diameter about 1 inch larger than your pie pan. To transfer a rolled-out piecrust to the pan, roll it up around the rolling pin, then unroll the crust into the pan. Open it and cut off excess, leaving $^1/_2$ inch extending beyond the edge.

(Recipe continues on next page.)

Fill with your favorite filling.

For a two-crust pie, repeat the above, and lay second crust over the filling, leaving 1 inch extending beyond the edge. Use a knife or pastry scissors to trim excess dough to 1-inch overlap. Tuck top overlap *under* the edge of the bottom crust.

Make a fluted edge by pinching the dough edge with thumb and forefinger of the left hand while pushing forefinger of the right hand between the pinch. Continue all around the pie. Cut slits in the top crust to release steam while baking. *(Jodi cuts eyes and mouth to make a happy face. Of course, when the juice dribbles out the slits, it looks like the happy face is either crying or slobbering.)*

Bake at required temperature for the filling (e.g., for apple pie, bake in an oven preheated to 450 degrees for 10 minutes, then turn down the temperature to 350 degrees for about 30 minutes or until the edges of the crust are golden brown).

Florida's Sweet Potato Pie

Florida says, "The recipe below is for one pie, but you better make two! Ya gotta have enough pie for all the drop-ins, know what I'm sayin'?"

2 lbs. or 2 to 3 sweet potatoes
1 stick butter ($\frac{1}{4}$ lb.)
2 eggs
1 cup brown sugar
1 $\frac{1}{2}$ cups soy milk or 1 can evaporated milk
1 tsp. vanilla
1 tsp. cinnamon
1 tsp. nutmeg
$\frac{1}{2}$ tsp. ginger
$\frac{1}{4}$ tsp. cloves
$\frac{1}{4}$ tsp. salt
Piecrust (see Jodi's Flaky Piecrust recipe)

Boil the sweet potatoes with the skins on until tender. Cool under running water until you can remove skins. Place the yams in a mixer and whip on medium speed, stopping occasionally to remove "strings" clinging to the beaters.

Add butter until melted and mixed. Then add the remaining ingredients and continue mixing until smooth. If the batter is too thick to pour, add additional soy milk until smooth.

Pour your batter into an unbaked pie shell, sprinkle a dash of cinnamon on the top, and bake for 50 minutes to 1 hour, or until

(Recipe continues on next page.)

brown specks appear on the surface of the pie and an inserted knife blade comes out clean.

Allow to cool at least 1 hour. It is also delicious chilled.

Serves 6 brothers or 8 "sistahs" on a diet.

Ruth's Potato Latkes

Simple to make, kids like them, and they're kosher! (Of course, if you have twins trying to "help" and the phone rings ... even "simple" has its limits.)

4 medium potatoes
1 medium onion or three scallions, finely chopped
2 eggs, beaten
$^3/_4$ cup matzo meal (bread crumbs or 3 tbsp. flour may be substituted)
1 tsp. salt
$^1/_4$ tsp. black pepper
$^1/_4$ cup fresh parsley, chopped (optional)
Vegetable oil for frying

Grate the potatoes into a large bowl. Discard any liquid. Stir in onions, salt, pepper, and parsley. Add the matzo, mixing well before stirring in the eggs.

Heat oil in a large frying pan. Use $^1/_4$ to $^1/_3$ cup of batter for each *latke*, spreading it with a fork into thin cakes about the size of your palm. Cook 4 to 5 minutes per side or until golden brown. Drain pan-fried latkes on paper towels. (Or heat a griddle to 350 degrees with just a spray of oil on it. Griddle latkes may not turn out so crispy, but they contain far less fat.)

Serve hot with a scoop of cold applesauce and a dollop of sour cream. Serves about 4.

If desired, accompany with sausages. *(But don't tell Ruth if they're not kosher.)*

U. S. TO METRIC CONVERSION TABLE

CAPACITY
$^1/_5$ teaspoon = 1 ml
1 teaspoon = 5 ml
1 tablespoon = 15 ml
1 fluid oz. = 30 ml
$^1/_5$ cup = 50 ml
1 cup = 240 ml
2 cups (1 pint) = 470 ml
4 cups (1 quart) = .95 liter
4 quarts (1 gal.) = 3.8 liters

WEIGHT
1 oz. = 28 grams
1 pound = 454 grams

Notes

1. From a letter written by colonist Edward Winslow, dated December 12, 1621, and published in *Mourt's Relations*, by George Morton, 1622, London.

2. "Ready My Heart," © 1976, Lois Farley Shuford. All rights reserved. Used by permission. Available on the CD by Steve Bell, *The Feast of Seasons*, © 1995 www.signpostmusic.com.

3. Latin hymn from the twelfth century, translated by John M. Neale, 1851. The original hymn had seven or eight verses. These four match the weekly themes best.

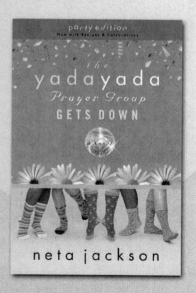

Each novel
now includes
numerous pages
of celebration
ideas and
recipes that flow
from the story

CPSIA information can be obtained at www.ICGtesting.com
Printed in the USA
LVOW04s0139100913

351589LV00006B/26/P

9 781595 543615